BOYFRIEND SEASON

KELLI LONDON

Dafina KTeen Books
KENSINGTON PUBLISHING CORP.
www.kensingtonbooks.com/KTeen

DAFINA KTEEN BOOKS are published by

Kensington Publishing Corp.
119 West 40th Street
New York, NY 10018

All Kensington titles, imprints, and distributed lines are available at special quantity discounts for bulk purchases for sales promotion, premiums, fund-raising, educational, or institutional use.

Special book excerpts or customized printings can also be created to fit specific needs. For details, write or phone the office of the Kensington Special Sales Manager: Attn. Special Sales Department. Kensington Publishing Corp., 119 West 40th Street, New York, NY 10018. Phone: 1-800-221-2647.

K logo Reg. US Pat. & TM Off.
Sunburst logo Reg. US Pat. & TM Off.

ISBN-13: 978-0-7582-6127-4
ISBN-10: 0-7582-6127-6

First Printing: August 2011
10 9 8 7 6 5 4 3 2 1

Printed in the United States of America

For my life's greatest joys:

Tweet

&

Que-Dog

&

Ky Boogie

Acknowledgments

A special thanks to my princess and princes: T, CII, and K. Without your love, patience, guidance, and being my three-person cheering squad none of my works would make it to completion.

An adoring welcome and hugs to my newfound prince, JJH.

JLH, Majesty begets Majesty, and Majesty needs Majesty. Here's to majestic bliss and love, and the unwavering love of Your Royal Highness, CLP.

For my family and friends who so willingly overlook and forgive me being missing in action while I'm writing, and keep me stocked with chocolates as an incentive to get the work done, I thank you.

A huge kudos and many hugs to my dream-team consultants in New York, Atlanta, and Philadelphia: Rukiya "Kiki" Murray, Alakea Woods, Josh "UnconQUErable" Woods, Chris Ferreras, and Eligio "E." (Zap) Bailey. You are all priceless!

Thanks to my fellow writers who offer wonderful teen readers an escape and entertainment, I am proud to be a part of the movement. Ni-Ni Simone, Kevin Elliott, and Shelia Goss, keep wielding your pens . . . okay, your computers!

Selena James, what can I say? A mere thanks is not enough. However, it'll have to do until the dictionary— or one of us writers—comes up with something more appropriate. So, thank you for the belief, the push, the encouragement, and the world introduction.

For my readers, I truly and humbly thank you with all of my heart. You're incredible, appreciated, and top of tops. Let's rock the world together!

From Kelli

When I sat down to write *Boyfriend Season*, three things quickly whirled through my mind besides the trio of characters I love, and hope you'll love as much. Those things are the selfs (self-everything that's positive, such as self-esteem, self-belief, self-confidence, etc.), power, and empowerment. The reasons for those propelling thoughts moving through my mind with the speed of my typing—and, trust your girl Kell on this, it sounds like popcorn popping when I'm on the computer, and my fingers appear blurry from a distance due to my lightning-quick keypad strokes—is because I believe all of us possess an inner greatness and beauty. However, our good qualities are oftentimes challenged, and if we're not careful, they're often dimmed.

So what do you do when your inner greatness and beauty are challenged, tested, and trialed? What do you do when your friends are doing something else, something you would rather not do or even approve of? What do you do when you choose not to go with the popular crowd because you are an individual with individual thoughts who faces individual circumstances? You rely on your positive selfs, that's what, because within you lies the power to make the right choices, to license yourself to be . . . well, you—the best you. And that, my dear reader, is total empowerment. Empowerment is your road.

So here's the deal—the real, down-low and dirty deal

on how to win at life. Believe in yourself. Trust yourself. Educate yourself. Go after any and every positive thing that you want, then capture it. Most importantly, love yourself. Love yourself hard and pure and to your very core, and make sure you like yourself along the way. And though it sounds cliché because it seems overused, you *can* be whatever you want. Life will be hard; I won't lie to you about that. Boyfriends will break your heart. Parents will be parents, and will seem as if their only mission in life is to dull your shine—but that's not the case. And some friends, you'll discover, aren't really friends at all, and there's no such thing as frenemies. There will be a lot of bumps and ditches, but there will and can be more smooth lanes and a zenith that's reachable. Don't believe me? Learn from my girls in *Boyfriend Season*.

Santana, Dynasty, and Patience are getting ready to go through a lot. And though their story is set in Atlanta, their issues are worldwide because, as you and I both know, every season is boyfriend season, and with boys oftentimes come problems and drama. Some we invite, some we're just presented with like that ugly piece of whatever we didn't ask for. Luckily, for us, problems usually have solutions.

If you ever have a problem that you can't fix, hit me up online. I'll help if I can.

Take care. Be strong. Love yourself.

Your girl,

Kells
www.KelliLondon.com

"All I need in my life of sin is me and my ~~girl~~friend" ^{boy}
—Jay-Z, "Bonnie and Clyde"
(Revision, Santana Jackson)

```
┌─────────────────────────────────────┐
│                                       │
│      SPECIAL INVITATION TO            │
│   THE HOTTEST SURPRISE PARTY          │
│        OF THE SUMMER                   │
│                                       │
│              For                       │
│                                       │
│        Santana Jackson                 │
│                                       │
│               +                        │
│                                       │
│          One Guest                     │
│                                       │
└─────────────────────────────────────┘
```

The invitation was in her hands. Between her fingers, and Santana couldn't believe it. Yes, she'd always been hot, one of the few who pulled everyone's attention, but now that her life had changed, she hadn't expected to be invited to the biggest rapper of all time's surprise birthday party.

She looked at her dress, and felt more than beautiful—she was exquisite. She scanned the crowd, and saw the people matched the feeling soaring through her. Yes, she was still on top. Then she looked to her right, and sized up the guy next to her. He was her date, and now everyone would know—everyone who expected her to be dangling on the arm of someone else. She hoped they'd all understand and celebrate her decision. It was summer, after all, and after spring bloomed change. Change of clothes, change of heart, change of mind—and especially change of boyfriends. If summer wasn't anything else, it was definitely boyfriend season.

```
┌─────────────────────────────────────┐
│                                      │
│      SPECIAL INVITATION TO           │
│   THE HOTTEST SURPRISE PARTY         │
│        OF THE SUMMER                 │
│                                      │
│              For                     │
│                                      │
│         Dynasty Young                │
│                                      │
│               +                      │
│                                      │
│          One Guest                   │
│                                      │
└─────────────────────────────────────┘
```

Dynasty gripped her invite, and held on to her date for balance. She wasn't used to high heels or standing on tiptoe in search of some boy. But the guy she was looking for was different. Super fine, he'd swaggered his way down from New York to Hotlanta, and stepped straight into her heart—just as she'd accidentally slipped into her date's—without trying. So was it her fault that she was digging one guy and had shown up at the most blazing party of the year with the one who dug her most? She shrugged. Her date was the greatest boy she knew, but they were friends. *Just best friends*, she told herself.

Fireworks exploded in the sky, catching Dynasty off guard. She jumped and almost fell. Then she saw him. The guy who had her heart. The same dude who had swaggered his way to Hotlanta and, apparently, into the heart of the girl he'd brought with him. Her name was Meka, and her swagger matched his. Dynasty blinked back her disappointment and swallowed her jealousy.

"You okay, Dynasty?" her date asked.

She looked at him, saw the beauty that lived behind his eyes, and thought, *isn't this what every girl wants—her boyfriend to be her best friend?* She had a decision to make, and she decided it'd be tonight. It was the party of the year and, for her, boyfriend season.

```
┌─────────────────────────────────────────┐
│                                           │
│        SPECIAL INVITATION TO              │
│      THE HOTTEST SURPRISE PARTY           │
│            OF THE SUMMER                   │
│                                           │
│                  For                      │
│                                           │
│           Patience Blackman               │
│                                           │
│                  +                        │
│                                           │
│              One Guest                    │
│                                           │
└─────────────────────────────────────────┘
```

Dear God. Thank you. Thank you so much, Patience prayed silently as lights flashed and microphones were thrust in her and her date's faces. She smiled a megawatt grin, and took in the positive energy surrounding her. Like the star everyone was now calling her, she stood tall on the red carpet with a real superstar next to her, and had not an ounce of remorse about leaving the one she'd left. She'd chosen the right guy as her date, she knew she did. So why was she so nervous about running into her ex? *Just nerves*, she told herself as anxiousness climbed her. She'd never been to a party before, hadn't ever attended a real concert, and now here she was, a church girl with an R & B/hip hop record who was surrounded by celebrities and Atlanta's it crowd. No, Sunday service hadn't prepared her for this, not her new life.

"'Ey! You look good, Patience," her cousin, Meka called through the crowd, pushing her way over.

Patience waved, and excused herself from her date.

"Hey to you, too," she greeted her rowdy, but fun-loving cousin, then turned to Meka's best friend she hadn't seen until they were closer. "Hi, Santana! You look wonderful."

Santana grabbed Patience by both wrists, bopped up and down, and cut her a coy look. "Who's looking fab, superstar? I heard your song on the radio. Hot to def! I mean, it sounds really good."

Patience pulled away, laughing. "Thanks. I tried to do a lil something-something."

Meka laughed. "Patience, it's sumthin' sumthin', not something something. Don't worry, you'll get it." She stopped talking, and began waving her arm frantically. "Hey Dynasty! Over here!" She turned to Patience. "Now this one you must meet. She's right up your alley. Good girl. Smart. Going places . . . and a little homely," she teased. "But you'll love her. I promise."

1

SANTANA JACKSON

Santana burst out of the classroom and into the hall. She couldn't take it anymore. Not the classroom. Not the students. Not the teacher or her rules. It was summertime. Boyfriend—Pharaoh—and boosting—clothes—season. She had things to do, and plenty of time as far as she was concerned. Well, at least now that she was skipping the rest of the day she did.

"This school can kiss my entire *asssk* me no questions and I'll tell you no lies!" Santana mumbled as loudly as she could, breezing past Beekman, the summer-school principal. She wanted him to hear her, just not be able to *prove* what she'd said. Cursing in the Atlanta public school system was forbidden—a major violation she thought ridiculous and refused to be penalized for. She didn't do detention, and had no plans of starting today.

She had more important things on her agenda like shopping and meeting her boyfriend, Pharaoh. Besides, if her mother didn't care what she said, who were the teachers to question what escaped her lips? Plus, being on lockdown in a classroom was raggedy with a capital R. But rappers, thugs, and corner boys—hustlers around her way who made things happen by connecting the dots—they were a different story. Who didn't want a dude who was saucy, could feed your pockets, stomach, and mind, and spat "shawty" through platinum and diamond grills covering his teeth?

Pausing in the middle of the hallway, Santana turned and mean-mugged Beekman, who'd quietly fallen in step behind her. She silently dared him to question her being in the almost desolate hallway during class time, then shrugged her shoulders in a what's-up-whatchu-wanna-do gesture. When she wasn't met with opposition, she mouthed *I didn't think so* to the principal's lack of action, then hoisted her book bag over her bra strap, swooped her index and middle fingers through her belt loops, and hiked up her too-tight jeans to cover her butt that Rashad, her neighbor, referred to as an onion. An apple. A badonka-donk that served as an asset in the hood. Then she exhaled, realizing she'd been holding her breath and that she had an audience. A smile tugged at the corners of her mouth when she noticed two boys staring. They were admiring what was beneath the denim separating their eyes from her juiciness, so she got her sway on, moved her hips like a pendulum while their eyes followed the switch of her hips. She was fly and knew it.

"A'ight, Santana!" they greeted with a head nod.

"Yep." Santana threw up the deuces and kept it moving. Yes, they knew her name, but so did just about everyone else in the school. She was Santana Jackson. Pharaoh's girl. And they were just fans.

Her phone vibrated in her purse as she pushed her weight against the door, exiting with a bang. It was almost one o'clock, close to their predetermined meeting time. Her feet lightened with each step as her shoes connected with the concrete beneath them. As always, she couldn't wait to see Pharaoh. Not only was he her dude, he was *the* man. His name rang bells, and his hood power preceded him. There wasn't anything that Pharaoh couldn't do—except Santana. She wasn't going to give in to him or be like one of the floozies who dropped their panties to guys because they were fly. She knew better and vowed to heed her mom's example: If you give a guy what he wants, he has nothing to stick around for, but if you give him just a smidge of what he wants, he'll stay for the rest.

" 'Bout time! I was just calling you. I thought I was gonna havta come up in there and jailbreak you," Meka Blackman, Santana's best friend, said, snapping closed her cell and leaning next to the door.

"I know, right? I tried to leave faster, but Principal Beekman was parading around like he running something, so I had to walk the halls for a minute," Santana answered as they left the grounds and turned the corner.

"So we scared of principals now?" Meka teased.

Santana shrugged and walked up to the passenger door of the borrowed pickup Meka was driving. "I ain't scared of nothing. But I'm not doing detention for nobody . . . especially not two days before summer school lets out—I'm not trying to risk doing a repeat. Ya heard?" Meka clicked open the locks with the car's alarm remote. Santana stepped up into the cab of the truck and asked, "How long you got this one?"

Meka stuck a key in the ignition, turned, and winked. Throwing the gear in DRIVE, she brick-footed the accelerator. "Until whoever's-this-is pays my brother. He must owe him big time 'cause the rims alone on this godda be at least ten stacks. Don't worry, I'll get you to your man on time. First we got biz to handle, though. Then after that I need to check on my cousin, Patience." The truck blew down the street on the ten-thousand-dollar rims, zooming faster than any speed limit in the country, blasting music. "You ready?"

Santana held on tight. "You mean your church cousin with all the money?"

Meka nodded, adjusting the radio dial.

"That's what's up. When's she hanging with us?"

Meka turned, and deadpanned. "Either when hell freezes over or heaven warms up. My uncle *The* Bishop Blackman ain't having it. He don't want our ways tarnishing his daughter!" She turned up the radio, nodding her head to the music.

"Turn that up! Is that Trill's new song, 'Talum'bout'? We godda cop us tickets to his next concert."

"Yeah . . ." Meka agreed, nodding her head to the song. "That's that ish." She turned up the radio. "Okay, enough. We got biz to handle." She muted the speakers when the hottest teen rapper's song went off.

"And I'm ready too. You got my silencer?" Santana asked, referring to her boosting bag, the one they'd lined with foil and magnets and others things that prevented store's security detectors from sounding off when they exited the store with stolen goods.

Meka smiled and took a sharp corner on Peachtree, headed toward Lenox Square Mall. "Nope. I didn't bring your silencer, sis. . . ."

Santana scowled.

". . . I brought you two. Your old one and a *new* one. Check in the back. Now fix your face! Over there looking like someone pissed in your cereal," Meka said, then laughed.

Santana joined her, then reached into the backseat of the truck and retrieved a big brown, recycled shopping bag. She was proud of her friend. "Even thieves are going green!" she teased.

"Ha-ha. I made some extras this morning 'cause I got orders to fill," Meka continued while Santana pulled a new tote from the brown bag.

"This the new Gucci? Jungle tote? The two-thousand-dollar jammie?" Santana's jaw fell in her lap while she admired the bag.

"Yep. *And* it's a silencer. Merry Christmas in the summertime. Don't say I ain't never give you nothing," Meka rattled. "ADT, Brinks . . . Atlanta Police Department—they can all kick rocks. Ain't no alarms gonna ring with all the stuff I lined our bags with!" She laughed and whipped into Lenox's parking lot.

Santana hugged Meka as soon as they hopped out of the truck.

Meka shrugged. "Don't be too happy. It's a knockoff, but no one can tell. Not even the employees that work at the store. Trust me. I returned one knockoff last week."

The M.A.C. counter was calling her name when they entered the mall and walked past Macy's, but she knew she didn't have time to stop. She was there to "shop" for a few items, maybe pick up some new Js, and then meet Pharaoh out front. He was due to pick her up in less than one hour.

"Where you wanna hit first?" Meka asked, smoothing out her sundress, then her extra short hair that was styled to perfection as usual. "You need a new Louis, right?"

Santana walked beside her, shouldering her dressed-up boosting bag and rocking her black and purple high-heeled Air Jordan 8s. There wasn't a soul who could tell her she wasn't a showstopper. Pausing in front of a store window, she checked her reflection. Fingering the top of her hair that was expertly spiked in a Mohawk, she turned sideways and admired how her graduated length cascaded down her back. *Even if I didn't grow this, no one can tell me my hair isn't fire.*

"I do, but wrong mall. Louis is in Phipps Plaza across the street. You always forget."

"Right. Phipps. Too expensive and too much security for me. I'm not trying to get locked up again," Meka answered, capping her lip gloss and putting it in her purse, signaling she was done and ready. "You're cute. Come on," she added, interrupting Santana's beauty session.

"I know. You too."

Meka grabbed her wrist, then pushed Santana's hair from her face. "What? When did you get these," she asked, fingering Santana's earrings. "These are ultra hot!"

Santana blushed. "Pharaoh had them made for me. If

you look carefully, you can see Ps in the design," she squealed, proud of her man.

"That's what's up. He's claiming his woman! Now it's time to get to work." Meka tilted her head; then they both nodded. If they were going to boost, they decided long ago that they'd better do it dressed to the hilt so they would be inconspicuous. Being raggedy would make security hawk them.

A crowd of dusty teenage boys walked past them and headed back toward the entrance of Macy's. Rundown sneakers, last season's clothes, jeans sagging too low and voices talking too loud, they were definitely targets for mall and department store security. They were also the distraction Santana and Meka needed to keep them under the radar.

"Guess Macy's it is," Santana said.

Silencer bag filled to capacity, Santana exited the third store they'd hit and headed toward the escalator. Her adrenaline rushed, her heart raced, and she was sure she was shaking. It took every ounce of willpower she had not to turn around to look to see if they were being followed. She was nervous. *Just nervous*, she told herself.

"We need to go upstairs. That's where the Js are," Santana said, leading Meka through the mall, past the Starbucks, and finally to the escalator. "One of us needs to buy something. I'm gonna cop the Js for Pharaoh." She stepped on the ascending stairs, then turned around so she could check their surroundings while she was speaking to Meka. "We're good. Nobody's thinking about us."

Meka's expression was twisted. "Why you buying Pharaoh something? Shouldn't it be the other way 'round?" she asked, hopping off and following Santana.

Santana laughed, then entered the store. "Girl, nah. He always buys me stuff. A pair of Js ain't nothing. Plus, for what I'll get in return . . . it's a good investment. Anyway, I want my man to look good."

"Don't keep him looking too good. You know them floozies at your school be after him. Especially Nae."

Santana sickened. She couldn't stand Nae, her ex-best friend who'd gone after Pharaoh at a party. "Meka, forget it. Don't even bring it up. He don't want Nae. How could he . . . after this?" Santana swung her weave while strutting over to the men's sneaker section. She grabbed the new Js and Ones off the display, then asked a salesperson to bring her a size-twelve pair of each.

"Hmmm. Don't ever say what ya man won't do. K?" Meka said, following Santana to the counter.

Santana turned on her three-inch-heel Jordans. "Why Meka? Is that a warning or a hint? You know something? Talk to your girl, Meka!" she said, peeling off a few big bills, paying for the sneakers.

Meka eyed the money.

"Courtesy of Pharaoh." Santana took the bags from the salesperson.

Meka walked out, shrugging. "I'm just saying, Santana. Don't ever be so sure. K? Nae may not be fire like you but, just like ya man, she gives courtesies too. Maybe not cash, but her courtesies rhyme with cash."

"And I'll kick her in hers if she tries me again," Santana pointed out as they exited the mall. "There's

Pharaoh's car over there. I'll call you later, Meka." She blew her best friend air kisses, then sashayed toward her man. " 'Ey, baby!" Santana waved and cheesed so hard she was sure her teeth would shatter. The wind swept her weave off her back and moved her closer to him.

Pharaoh played with the chew stick in his mouth, biting and turning and sucking on it as if it were sugarcane. He gave Santana a head nod, reached over and opened her door.

"S'up, shawty? You lookin' kinda right in dem there jeans."

Shaking her head, she put her bags in the backseat and suppressed the melting feeling that swept through her every time he was near. Pharaoh had a way of appealing to her senses, starting with his street talk. Everything he said, no matter how simple, was beautiful to her because she loved his ghetto-fabulous country grammar. Sliding into the seat next to his, Santana leaned her weight to the left until her shoulder touched his, then wrapped her arms around him and met his lips with hers, giving him a sweet peck. They could've shared a seat and, still, she couldn't be close enough.

"Thanks. You what's up. Where're we going?"

Pharaoh roared the Charger's engine and spread his soft lips into a sneaky smile, revealing a platinum and rose-gold grill.

"Er'where Shawty. Ya know? If you still rollin'." He threw the gearshift in drive, released the brake, and accelerated until their heads indented the headrests like they were on a roller coaster.

Santana powered down her window, letting the warm

Atlanta air flow in and the blaring music out. She bopped her head, reached over, and ran her palm over his arm, loving the way his skin felt on hers. It was intoxicating knowing how powerful her man was. *There's nothing he can't do.* T.I. was rapping in the background. Paper-bag brown, fresh low cut with natural waves, he had just the slightest under bite that made his chin jut forward, causing him to look hard all the time. She took her hand, rubbed it over the hair he was growing on his chin.

"What up? You don't like that, shawty?" He looked over, flashed a slight crooked-tooth smile that revealed his platinum lower teeth, then stopped the car at the red traffic light.

She blushed. "You know I do." She reached in the back, retrieved the bag with his fresh kicks in it, then handed it to him.

He accepted the bag, then looked in it. He opened it and pulled out the Nike box first. A smile surfaced, followed by a low laugh. He nodded. "That's why I'm wit you, shawty. You a good girl and you know what it is. That's why I got a surprise for you too. Stick wit ya man, baby, and we going everywhere. Straight to the top, shawty."

2

DYNASTY YOUNG

Dynasty was tired of the nonsense. Super exhausted of her surroundings and the people who inhabited them—inside the apartment and out of it. Especially her only friend, Rufus, whose underwear had been in a twist ever since she ignored his crushing on her, and had made it a point to try to get under her skin any way he could. She shook her head. She couldn't wait to escape, and she would. Her dictionary would be key in her breaking free, she believed, mentally repeating the definitions her ever-expanding lexicon required she feed her brain.

"Dy-nas-tee. Dyyy-nasty! Die nasty. Die nasty!" Rufus's insults blew through her opened bedroom window from one floor down.

Dynasty pulled back the dull white sheer and stuck her head out into the warm sunshine.

"You better get away from here, Rufus. Or I'm gonna

come down and split your head with a brick. You hear me?" she spat, teasing and almost hating that she'd ever taken time out of her life to be nice to her mentally challenged neighbor. Rufus wasn't really handicapped; he'd just started to act like he was when she wouldn't kiss him—which was grosser than gross since they'd been close forever, and she viewed him more like family than anything else. *Well, at least I did*, she thought. They'd only hung out exclusively for a couple of months—as friends—and he'd acted as if they were a couple. She shook her head. She couldn't understand Rufus, or why he was so upset. She'd never treated him like they were together.

"What you gonna do? Hit me with that dictionary you always reading? Come down and do it," six-foot-five Rufus dared, his voice gruff and deep like a man twice his age. Everything about Rufus was to the second power. His height. Weight. Neediness and attitude. Ever since he'd been put on steroids for his rumored heart condition he'd vehemently denied having for months before she made him spill the truth, he'd ballooned like a jellyfish and wore his insecurity like a cape he thought was invisible. Dynasty could see it, though, because with each rejection from either neighborhood homeboys or some silly girl, it grew thicker and more apparent, and she was always the one to cheer him up.

"You better get your short-yellow-bus-riding behind away from my window, Rufus! Or I'm gonna have my brother handle you." She stepped aside, making sure he didn't see her, and covered her laughter. She didn't really want to scare Rufus, but he'd been so mean lately she thought a little shaking up might do him some good. She moved back in his sight.

Rufus looked up and met her stare with his. He flipped up his middle finger. "That's why you ain't never gonna get into that rich-people school you keep studying to get in. And I ain't worried about nobody handling me. Why don't you have your man do it? Your brother's not—"

"You're just jealous that I didn't choose you, and, for your information, my brother will be home from jail *this* week. Wanna try me, Ruthless Rufus?" Dynasty challenged, using one of the nicknames he hated and the only thing she had to help save her from Rufus's verbal attack—her brother King's killer reputation. But the truth was her brother was never getting out of jail and her mother was probably never getting off of heroin and she'd probably never get a scholarship to Winchester Hills Prep, her ticket to a good college.

"Yeah. A'ight," Rufus said. "But you know you dead wrong, Dynasty. I know you was messing around with J.R. last night. You kissed him . . . *and* some. I'm not telling you what I heard; I'm telling what he told me. That's why you gonna die nasty and young, Dynasty Young!" he barked, then disappeared down the block.

"Whatever. You're lying. J.R. didn't tell anything like that. Couldn't of. And you know what else, Rufus? You make my butt itch!" she said, reaching behind her and pulling a wedgie out—something she had to do often because of the booty shorts she rocked most of the summer. "So go! Get outta here looking like a rejected remix of Biggie Smalls and Fat Albert. You just mad I didn't want you and you couldn't pull me, Rufus! This madness is juvenile! One minute we're cool, the next your 'tude is popping. You keep acting like we're not friends." She mumbled the last sentence to his back, knowing every other word she'd said cut into him. He was a *troglodyte*—an unlearned person without culture, the word she'd committed to memory last week. So his ignorant-acting ways weren't his fault, she reminded herself. She really didn't like hurting him, but he forced her to, and it made her feel terrible, because deep down she liked him as a friend.

Closing the sheer curtain, Dynasty stepped away from the window, then settled onto the old mattress that served as her bed, careful not to fall onto her prized dictionary. She was tired of battling the likes of Rufus and other project dudes like him. She sucked her teeth, looking around her tiny dingy room. She hated her surroundings and wasn't too fond of the people who inhabited them. Stuck in Thomasville Heights, a fenced-in Atlanta housing project complete with a guarded gate and a penitentiary around the corner, she was reminded daily that girls like her weren't expected to go far in life.

She rolled her eyes at her forecasted future, sickened by who society said she'd become if she didn't escape the projects and the madness. *The Withouts*. Half of the grown-ups she knew were The Withouts; they were either *without* an education or most of their teeth. Sometimes both. Most of the teens weren't too far behind.

"Dynasty!" her Aunt Maybelline called from downstairs. "Get down here!"

Speaking of no teeth. Dynasty pushed herself up from the cheap mattress and made haste out of the room, stepping over the dirty clothes, clean clothes, and some other accessories that belonged on a person, not a floor, and made it down the steps. She was thankful she didn't wound her bare feet and chastised herself for forgetting her slippers. Aunt Maybelline kept a nasty house and wouldn't let her clean anything but her room.

"Ma'am?" she answered her aunt with as much respect as she could manage.

Aunt Maybelline just stared through the cloud of smoke that floated around her head, then flicked her cigarette on the coffee table, looking very deserving of her name. Drawn-on eyebrows. Inch-long eyelashes thickly coated with five coats of mascara. Enough eyeliner to trace a map of the U.S. was surrounded by pools of blush and a cherry-red lipstick that bled past her lip line. Dynasty shook her head. *I live with Bozo. A clown.* Her aunt flicked her ashes again, this time on top of an unopened carton of cancer sticks, not even bothering to aim for the ashtray or caring about Dynasty's asthma.

"Ma'am?" Dynasty asked again, eyeing a case of beer sitting on top of the coffee table alongside the cigarette carton.

Aunt Maybelline reached in her parachute-sized bra and retrieved a damp-looking ten-dollar bill. She handed it to Dynasty.

"Go to the store and get me some cigarettes and a twelve-pack."

Dynasty crinkled her nose and knew Aunt Maybelline hadn't taken her medication. There were twenty-four beer cans and two-hundred cigarettes on the coffee table and her aunt was trying to send her to the store? *Man. She can't be serious.*

"Auntie, you already have beer and cigarettes. Plus, ten dollars isn't enough and you know they won't let me buy that stuff. I'm only thirteen," she lied, deciding to get some entertainment for the day since Rufus had an attitude and wasn't up for making her laugh.

Aunt Maybelline reared back her head. "Fourteen."

Dynasty looked her in the eyes, knowing her aunt didn't know if she was thirteen or thirty.

"No, Auntie. *Thir*teen," she lied again.

"*Thirteen*? Since when? Humph. That means we got five years left," her aunt said, referring to how long the state would kick in money and a food-stamp card to aid her aunt in raising her.

Dynasty nodded, knowing full well she was fifteen. "Today, Aunt Maybelline. I turned thirteen today so I can't buy beer and cigarettes."

"Oh. Well. Happy thirteenth. When you find somebody to help you buy my drink, we'll toast." Aunt Maybelline shrugged. Still staring, she pulled her cigarette again and blew the smoke in Dynasty's face. "Go. Get. My. Cigarettes. And. Twelve-pack. I'm almost out, and Pork Chop's coming over so we can celebrate his grandson coming to stay with him from New York," she hissed, serious as ever and clipping her words.

Dynasty reached out, handing back the nasty, damp ten-dollar bill. Aunt Maybelline slapped her hand so hard it stung, then kicked off her prized pair of old-school bright green jelly shoes with the backs cut out.

"Take ya butt now, and wear these. And ya better bring back my cigarettes, twelve-pack, *and* my shoes. I know you and ya raggedy friends been scheming on my shoes. You and that friend of yours, that big, black boy. I see y'all looking."

"Auntie—" Dynasty began, deciding to try to reason with Aunt Maybelline one last time.

"*Auntie,* my foot. Go or find you someplace else to stay. Make a way—and wear my shoes so I know you'll have to come back."

Dynasty put her feet in the awful bright-green jelly shoes and walked out the door. In the warmth of the sunshine, she exhaled and prayed no one saw her. Never mind that she had on orange, wearing different colors didn't bother her half as much as rocking shoes nearly five sizes too big. That, she didn't want anyone to see.

"Mm. Mm. Mm," loudly penetrated the quiet air, forcing Dynasty to turn around.

"Hey Sheeka!" she called out to the neighborhood kitchen beautician who could hear but couldn't speak.

Sheeka pointed to Dynasty's hair, then raised her hands in the air.

Dynasty shook her head in the negative. "No, Sheeka. I don't have money to get my hair done, but when I do I'll check for you."

Sheeka looked at Dynasty's feet, then up to her face. She shook her head, then walked away.

"Shuckey duckey," Rufus sang from afar, walking up on her seconds after Sheeka departed. "Them there shoes are hot, Dynasty!" He laughed.

She really rolled her eyes now. Hard. "Not now, Rufus. Okay?"

Rufus stood next to her, shading her like a tree. "What happened, shawty? Aunt Maybelline didn't make it to the pharmacy, huh? Well, maybe your man J.R. will buy you some shoes you can fit . . . with all that corner-boy money he be banking."

Dynasty started sliding forward. She couldn't walk without tripping, so she slid her way toward the store. She regretted confiding in Rufus that her aunt was bipolar.

"Shut up, Rufus. You know that hurts my feelngs."

"Don't be mad at me," he said, scratching his ashy arms. "Better be glad she ran out of medicine 'cause if she didn't you'd probably be sleeping on the steps again until I come get you like the last time. I don't know why you don't just leave. You know she don't want you there. You ain't nothing but a check . . . or maybe . . ." he said, his tone changing into one laced with sarcasm. "You can sleep over J.R.'s. Oops. I guess you did that already, huh?"

Here we go again. He was trying to hurt her and she knew it. She stopped, turned, and looked up. Rufus couldn't comprehend *rational* and wouldn't entertain being *sagacious*—two of her dictionary words for the week, meaning reasonable and perceptive. She'd have to meet his childishness with the same.

"Anybody ever tell you that you're too big to be outside, Rufus? You're blocking the sun. Why are you so big, Dufus Rufus? And how you get so ashy when it's humid out? That's what's wrong. You mad 'cause my boyfriend isn't fat or ashy. Right?" She stared, waiting for an answer. "Rhetorical question. Oops. Sorry." She tilted her face sideways, then scratched her head. "You don't know what that means, huh? I forgot. You're fat, ashy, *and* stupid. But never mind that, Rufus. You know what I'd really like to know? How do you manage to be ashy—which comes from dryness—and musty—which comes from sweating—at the same time?"

Rufus bit his bottom lip, squinted his eyes, and flared his nostrils. He was getting mad now and it showed. Because he was so insecure about his weight it was easy for Dynasty to strike his nerve.

"Shut the eff up! 'For I hurt you," he snapped, then quickly looked away and hung his head. "You better be glad I like you 'cause if somebody else talked to me like that I'd hurt them for real."

Dynasty just laughed, knowing he was fronting; he wasn't going to harm her. If anything, he'd protect her. He had many times before. She walked over to him, managed to stand on her tiptoes, and planted a kiss on his cheek. Then she left him there, huffing and puffing and whining and cursing her name, and proceeded to slide the too big jelly shoes toward the gate so she could go to the store.

"Later, Rufus!" She waved.

Swoosh. Clap. Swoosh. Swoosh. Clap. She was having the hardest time maneuvering in Aunt Maybelline's jelly shoes. Finally, she rounded the corner and the exit was in sight. Suddenly she froze. *Dang.* Reluctantly, she checked her clothes, knowing nothing had changed since she'd practically been chased out the house. A tangerine, aqua, white, and yellow halter top was tied around her neck. Orange booty shorts clung to her rail-thin frame. Bright green jellys housed unpolished toes. She shook her head, then reached up. Sure enough, she still had a purple scarf tied around her head. *Talk about Aunt Maybelline? I must look like a clown, too. At least I didn't plan on going outside.* She tried to make herself feel better. But she was outside and so was he. The same *he* Rufus was mad about. J.R., short for Just Right.

" 'Ey!" J.R. yelled to a group of passersby, shaking his hand as if he were shooting dice. "Come see me next time." He held up two bottles of water. "Stop going to that store. I got what you need right here." He was on the other side of the street with his homeboy, feet from the guarded gate like he worked for the projects.

Dynasty tried to quicken her step, but the shoes slowed her down and were making too much noise. Wilting her head, she moved with purpose, carefully but surely, trying to act as if she was looking for something while she made tracks. She didn't want J.R. to see her and tried to convince herself that he wouldn't if she turned her attention to the ground or looked the other way. Big mistake.

" 'Ey!" he yelled.

She kept sliding forward, squinting in the burning sunlight.

" 'Ey! Dynasty!"

She stomped and picked up her head. *Dang.* She turned to her right, played it off, and waved.

"I godda go to the store. I'll be right back," she answered as loud as she could, hoping he'd hear her.

He waved her over. "Come here. Dynasty! Come here."

Dynasty shook her head in defeat. J.R. had a reputation for messing with pretty girls. Pretty girls who dressed nice. Pretty girls who dressed nice and had banging Coca-Cola-bottle bodies. She didn't fit into any of those categories. She looked down at herself one more time before crossing over, wondering what he'd seen in her last night. Her gaze traveled straight to her feet with no interruptions. She had not a hint of breasts to break up the view, just a case of the flats. Flat chest. Flat butt. Flat feet. And no hips to speak of. That's why it was so easy for her to get wedgies, she reasoned. *'Cause there's no cushion to stop my panties from creeping and crawling.*

"Hey." She waved as she crossed. "Don't look at what I got on. My Auntie—"

"Dang!" J.R.'s homeboy laughed. "You got dressed in the dark, shawty?"

J.R. waved his boy's comment away. "Nah! Don't worry, shawty. It's all good. Maybelline didn't take her medication again?" he asked, flashing her with a smile. "I know. I can tell. Ain't ya fault. So what's up later?"

Dynasty looked at him, then reared back her head a little. How did he know about Aunt Maybelline's condition? She hadn't told him. She shook her head. She was going to hang Rufus when she caught him.

"So . . . s'up later?" he repeated, speeding up his speech until *what's up* turned into one word, *s'up.*

Dynasty snapped out of her daze and stared. J.R. was cute at night, but he was finer in the daytime. Definitely out of her league. He was a come-up for her. Wife beater, saggy shorts, and a pair of brand-new white tennis shoes, were only outdone by the fresh braids he had hanging down his back. For a millisecond she felt a tinge of jealousy wondering whose legs he'd sat between to get his cornrows tightened. They weren't like that last night.

"I'm outside like this 'cause my aunt sent me on a wild mission to get her some cigarettes and beer." She shook her head. "They're not gonna let me buy that at the store."

J.R. waved his hand. "Ain't nuthin' to it, shawty. I can get that for ya."

Dynasty's eyes stretched into saucers. "Really?"

He nodded. "What's my name, shawty?"

"J.R."

"Naw. My name?"

"Just Right," she sang, admiring him.

"That's right. I'm just right about mine, and you mine, right? I mean after last night . . . can't be no other way." He nodded while he spoke and moved his hands a thousand miles an hour.

Dynasty grinned. She didn't know what else to do. She officially had a boyfriend. Just Right. *Me and Just Right.* She couldn't wait for Rufus to see them together so he wouldn't tease her anymore. She wouldn't need to threaten him with her brother who wasn't ever coming home anymore, and he'd finally believe that someone besides him was interested in her. Yes, he'd stop. Just Right had a reputation, too. Suddenly, something in her clicked that she didn't like.

"What do you mean by 'after last night'? What happened last night?"

J.R. smiled. "Come on, Dynasty. I don't put my business out there."

"Okay!" His boy held his fist up to his mouth and coughed the word into his hand. " 'Ey. Just Right. We godda go. Now! P-Down's pulling in too."

Just Right looked past Dynasty, then back at her. "Give me the money and meet me at the store. By the time you get there, I'll be walking out with your stuff. A'ight?"

Dynasty saw P-Down pull up on the left, then turned and saw a group of pretty girls walking up behind her. Pretty girls who dressed nice. Pretty girls who dressed nice and had banging bodies.

"Why can't I just go with you?" she asked, wondering if he'd lied on her like Rufus said. His boy seemed to know something she didn't.

"You don't wanna ride with P-Down. The car may be a lil hot or something. You know?"

She nodded and handed him the money, appreciating his help. She knew Aunt Maybelline was serious about putting her out if she didn't come home with the goods. *I have a boyfriend. A real boyfriend who helps me*, she thought as she slid out of the project, made a right, and proceeded to the corner store happier than she'd been in a long time.

Leaning against the barred window, she looked toward the street, waiting for J.R. and his boys to show, wondering how she'd beat them there. She was sure she'd been at the store at least ten minutes. The heat on her face and the sweat raining down her back told her so. She turned around, pushed herself up on tippy toes, and cupped her hands on either side of her eyes, then pressed them to the glass and looked inside the store at the clock on the wall.

She'd been there fifteen minutes. She was just starting to worry when she turned and saw Just Right and his boys turn the corner in the car. A smile spread on her face and any doubts she carried disappeared. Her boyfriend wasn't going to let her down. She raised her hand to wave, then her smile faded. Just Right and his boys sped down the street with a car full of the pretty girls she'd just seen walking her way and Aunt Maybelline's ten dollars. Never once did Just Right look her way, but his boy blew the horn and waved.

"What am I gonna do now?"

3

PATIENCE BLACKMAN

Patience speed walked to the front of the church amidst the seventy or so parishioners who paraded toward the Bishop's outstretched hands. They all needed prayer, but not as much as she did. Not in her mind. But the difference between her and the churchgoers was she needed him to pray for her to save *her* from *him*—her father, and his strict rules. In one move, her hands clasped together and her knees bent as she dropped to them, closing her eyes.

"Dear God, please get me out of here!" Patience begged with bowed head. "No VH1. MTV. BET. Hip-hop. R & B. Fiction. Love Stories. *True Blood*. Boys. Facebook. Skype. Social networking of any kind. Not even my first cousin, Meka, or sister-girl friends of any kind outside of these walls. I can't do or have anything worldly, not even sing a tune—that's what he said, God. Nothing worldly . . .

and I think everything should be considered worldly because you made everything in this world. Maybe I'm too literal, but I don't get it," she whispered her prayers into her clasped fingers alongside other members who'd come to the front for special prayer, then looked up and saw her dad on the pulpit holding out his splayed fingers toward the few members upfront, then the thousands of parishioners in the stadium seats while he prayed over them like he was the shepherd and they the sheep.

He was crazy, Patience believed. How could he not want her to partake of anything of this world when the expensive suit he wore was of this world and not ... say ... the world of Jupiter? Or was she supposed to parade around naked? she wondered. That was, after all, how God had intended her to be. Otherwise, she wouldn't have been born that way. And what about all that "casting the first stone" stuff? Wasn't her father indirectly teaching her to judge others by telling her to keep away from anyone who wasn't saved or was of a different faith or had strayed from the straight and narrow?

Patience unfolded her body from its position in front of the pulpit and surveyed her surroundings. People and cameras and lights and microphones and speakers and more people, cameras, lights, and microphones and speakers filled the stadium-sized church while music played. Thousands upon thousands of people hung on to her father's every word, as if he only spoke heaven's law and he wasn't human. He wasn't viewed as just a man. He was a messenger and worshipped.

"Psst. Psst, " someone hissed for her attention.

Patience followed the "Psst" to where her mother was sitting. "Get back down and pray. Look like you're praying. The cameras. The cameras!" her mother whispered.

You're Bishop's daughter. What will the world think if you're not paying attention at service—and on camera, at that! What, you want to be a worldly girl like your cousin, Meka? Always hanging in the street? Patience knew that's what her mother would've said if she could, like so many times before.

Patience almost rolled her eyes. And she would have if it weren't for the nationally televised service, her respect for other church members, and the fact that, despite her resentment for her parents' twisted way of non-parenting, she still honored them as her elders and providers and was a true believer herself—in God, not religion. If she could, she was sure she'd have twisted her eyes in their sockets until she looked like something from a sci-fi movie trying to hypnotize someone. After that, she definitely would have stood up in front of the pulpit, hiked up her dress, bent over, and then patted her behind— inviting all the hypocrites to kiss where her father was doing any and everything he could to prevent the sun from shining. She glanced back over her shoulder one last time, wondering if she should just go for it. After all, she was going to hell anyway. That's what he'd told her this morning before church when he caught her singing a "worldly" song about love, but Patience knew better. Her father was just mad because he felt the song's artist had abandoned religious music—and his church—for an R & B music career.

"It's easier for a camel to pass through the eye of a needle than a rich man . . ." her father's melodic voice began preaching Matthew's gospel.

Patience rose up on her knees then, grinning and clapping, looking as if she were participating in the service. *Well, at least I'm not going to hell alone. Daddy, you're coming too. You're filthy rich, filthy, and rich. Three different things, Daddy. Three.* She looked out into the congregation, searching for her older sisters, Hope and Faith, hoping they hadn't left yet. They had driven a separate car and were her ticket to leaving early. She didn't want to stay for six or seven hours more, then have dinner with a bunch of hangers-on who probably wouldn't give their family the time of day if her father wasn't famous.

Her eyes scanned the crowd before landing on a familiar face. A person she'd been warned to stay away from—the daughter of the singer with the beautiful voice she'd been chastised for listening to this morning. Her one and only best friend in the whole world, Silky.

Silky cut her eyes at Patience and motioned her head toward an exit, then pointed ever so slightly. She shrugged.

Patience took the hint, faintly nodded and held up her hand. She splayed her fingers and rocked side to side to the rhythm of the soft music wafting from the speakers. To anyone else it would've appeared that she was just feeling the spirit and the beautiful music, but she was signaling to Silky that she'd meet her by the exit in five minutes.

Pushing through the heavy door as quietly and inconspicuously as she could, Patience almost screamed when she saw her best friend standing on the other side. When the door closed behind her and she was sure no one was watching, she grabbed Silky and wrapped her in a bear hug.

"Where've you been?" Patience asked, near squealing.

Silky jumped up and down, her voice rising like a stuck pig. "Oh God!" She grabbed Patience's cheeks in her hands. "I missed you, girl. Why haven't you returned my calls?" She slapped her thigh when she asked her question, an indication that she was serious.

"I didn't know you called." No one told her Silky had phoned, but it didn't surprise her. Her sisters had their respective cells and she didn't. Anyone who called her would have to get past her parents or the house staff. And if the bishop said not to put Silky through, the staff wasn't going to risk their jobs.

"What you mean? Never mind. Girl, I've been calling and calling and calling. I've been on the road with my mom since it's summertime. I even tried to Skype you. Bishop still won't let you sign up for it, huh? No Facebook or nothing?" She shrugged. "Anyway, I got you lots of things from the road. You wouldn't believe how cheap things are overseas."

Patience dropped her chin. She was embarrassed and ashamed and felt like a huge liar and backstabber. Silky didn't know Patience wasn't allowed to hang with her anymore, and Patience didn't have the heart to tell her. It was all her father's doing, and that was one of the reasons she couldn't stand him.

"Did you? Thank you, Silky. I'm so excited for you and your mom! I heard her on the radio this morning," Patience whispered loudly. "Girl, I almost passed out. I was sooo happy, she sounds sooo good."

Silky tossed her hair over her shoulder and pursed her heavily glossed lips—two things she didn't have before her mom became a star. Made up or not, she was beautiful inside and out, and that's what Patience loved about her. Weave or no weave. Makeup or none, Silky was genuine.

"So you wanna see our house? It's way better than the apartment. You've got to come, Patience. Got to." She jumped up and down in place. "We can't be friends thirteen out of fourteen years and you flake on me—not you of all people. We're like sisters. . . . Mom got you your own bed and everything." Silky rotated her neck, flashed her teeth, and stuck out her tongue. "So what you say? Huh? Please! Please! It's not too far from you, maybe thirty minutes away. I got a surprise for you."

Patience looked around the hallway. Her parents and grandparents were inside the sanctuary. Hope and Faith were nowhere to be seen, probably had left long ago. She shrugged. Why not? If no one in her family saw her with Silky could they ever say she was really with her? No.

"Of course I'm coming!"

"That's my girl!" Silky took a cell phone from her purse and began texting.

"Is that a BlackBerry?" Patience asked.

Silky twisted her face and started laughing. She continued texting. Her fingers moving faster and faster. "Girl, yeah. You don't have one?"

Patience shook her head.

Silky looked up. "I'm surprised. Everybody has one."

Patience winced. Silky's words stung. She was sure her friend hadn't meant to rub it in her face, but, still, it hurt because her not having a BlackBerry like everybody else made her feel like she wasn't down—like she was an outcast who couldn't fit in. She was always treated like an outsider who the inner circle wouldn't allow inside, all because she was Bishop Blackman's daughter. It was hard being a famous preacher's child, especially when a lot of your schoolmates attended your church, and many were scared that their wrongdoings would get back to their parents. So by default—her dad—she'd been misjudged a possible snitch.

Silky stuck her arm through Patience's and walked her out the door. "Come on!"

Patience dug her feet in the carpet. "Shouldn't we wait for your mom?"

"Girl, puh-leez. No. We'll see her soon. You just worry about your surprise," Silky answered, still walking and pulling.

Patience took one last look around and saw that all was clear. She grabbed Silky's wrist. "Follow me then. This is the best way out over here. No cameras."

By the time they made it to the parking lot, Patience doubled over to catch her breath. Panting, she stood up straight and speed walked toward a parked van. She couldn't just stand on the sidewalk and wait for Silky's mom to exit the church. She couldn't take a chance on getting caught.

"Why we hiding back here?" Silky asked, careful not to lean on the dirty van.

Patience just looked at her. "You haven't been on tour that long. Two, three months tops. You know Bishop doesn't play. Service isn't over yet."

"Right. Right. It's been two months," Silky said, then grabbed Patience's hand again. "Run low. . . . I can't wait for you to see your surprise!" she squealed and directed as she pulled Patience through the parking lot, past dozens of cars. "I seen our ride just pull in."

Patience zigzagged behind Silky, still crouching. She never realized that Silky referred to her mother as their ride. She just followed suit like she always did.

"Here we go." Silky ran up to a black SUV with tinted windows and opened the door. "Jump in before some-body sees!"

Without thinking or looking, Patience hopped into the backseat of the SUV. Still crouching for fear of being seen, she tucked her head between her knees and directed her stare to the floor. The sound of Silky slamming the door shut made her relax a little until a pungent smoke assaulted her nose. *Her mom doesn't smoke.* Stiffening, Patience sat up and her eyes bulged. One seat faced an-other, drawing her attention to two things she'd missed; they were in a stretch SUV and they weren't alone. Four guys were in the truck too, and they had bottles of alco-hol, gold teeth, tons of jewelry, and what she assumed to be a bag of an illegal drug that looked like sage.

Silky just smiled, wrapped her arm around some dude who sat in the middle of two others, and said, "Surprise! This one's for you, Patience."

The SUV almost took flight as the driver laid his foot on the accelerator.

4

SANTANA

Straight to the top my behind, Santana thought, sucking her teeth. Pharaoh could go kick rabbit turds as far as she was concerned. She was PO'd to the highest level of pisstivity. She crossed her arms and twisted in the passenger seat. How could he promise her a surprise and tell her *stick wit ya man,* then leave her in the car waiting for him for almost two hours—in the summertime heat, on a dangerous street known for drug trafficking and gang violence? If she didn't love him so much—if he didn't have a reputation for being more dangerous than the street he'd left her waiting for him on—she'd slap his platinum grill out of his mouth.

"He must not know I'm from the skreets." She pulled her phone from her purse, logged into Facebook, and thought about changing her relationship status to single, but it wasn't that serious and would make the nasty female dogs who wanted her man—namely Nae—come after him hard, and she didn't feel like battling the buzzards coming in for a kill. No one was going to dead her relationship with Pharaoh. *No one.*

"Gross," she said, wincing at the updates populating the screen. Namely, HotNsexy Jackson. HotNsexy Jackson was her too-young-to-be-called-Mom mother, who'd demanded they be Facebook friends, and she'd just made Santana's stomach turn by changing her relationship status and further informing the world that not only was she was in love, but also moving the man in.

"Not another one," Santana said, switching to her profile screen and wondering how long her mother would keep this new man Santana had never met but would be sharing a roof with.

"He godda have tall bank." Her mother had a bad habit of not keeping men, so Santana wasn't fazed. Her thoughts moved right back to Pharaoh. She moved the cursor to the text box next to her own status and clued the universe in on how she felt.

LUVZ A 4 LETTA WORD. SUMTYMZ IT'Z A CURSE, LIKE F-U, SUMTYMZ IT'Z A FEELIN. & AZ M@D AZ WE M@KE E@CH OTHER @ TYMZ, WE F-N LUV E@CH OTHER! LOL!!! E@T TH@T, H8TRZ!!! LOL!!!

She turned her phone around, pulled her hair back from her ears to show off the custom earrings that he'd bought her, snapped a picture of herself next to the headrest that had *Pharaoh* embroidered on it, then loaded it as her new profile picture. In seconds, her cell chimed twice. Texts from her mother and Meka.

GET, GET, GET IT! CRAIG SAYS HELLO DAUGHTER.

YO STATUZ IZ SWEET! HAV FUN. CALL ME L8TRZ

Santana rolled her eyes and the windows down. She wasn't having fun; she was bored and much too fly to be waiting on a dude. Didn't he know that by now? Sticking her head out, she surveyed the block, saw that it was relatively empty, wrapped her hand around the handle, and opened the passenger door.

"Oh so y'all in love! Ain't that sweet!" A girl's voice called out from the driver's side before Santana could put her foot on the ground.

Santana whipped her face around and saw a car full of hoodrats and chickenhead girls packed like sardines in a raggedy excuse for a car. One of them stood out from the rest, the one with the biggest mouth and attitude. Nae.

"Oh, *our* boyfriend got you mad?" Nae mocked in a toddler voice. "What happened, you still acting like you too good to go all the way, and now he's actin' up?"

Fire shot though Santana's veins. "You know what, Nae? You can go 'head wit all that. You know you don't want none of this. Don't try to act all bad cuz you got company. *My* boyfriend is just that, *mine*."

The girls in the car laughed, egging Nae on. "Bet next time you won't be Facebooking all yo bizness. Bet you didn't realize your picture showed what skreet you on!"

"Get her, Nae. . . . We ain't bring you here just to talk."

Nae chimed right in. "Well *your* boyfriend was *mines* last night. And I was so, so good to him. Do he tell you dat too? Dat you good to him? Do this sound familiar: 'Oh, oh, I can't believe I slept on you. I shoulda got wit you a long time ago, shawty,'" Nae said, deepening her voice to sound like Pharaoh.

That was it. Santana had had enough of backstabbing Nae. She took off her earrings, adjusted her rings to face forward so they could dig into Nae's skin when she punched her in the face, and hopped out of the car. Nae's butt kicking was long overdue, and Santana was the one to hand it to her.

They'd been friends once, or at least that's what Santana had believed until she got with Pharaoh. After that, Nae had started tripping, acting envious, and "accidentally" telling Pharaoh about boys Santana talked to when he wasn't around, but never telling him that Santana always kicked down their advances. Then Nae's envy turned to jealousy, and she no longer just desired to have things *like* Santana's, she wanted *what* Santana had—including Pharaoh. But she'd have to take him if she wanted him, and it wouldn't be easy. Santana could brawl with the best of them, and Nae wasn't even close to best or any word starting with a *B* but one, and it ended in itch—exactly what the wounds Santana planned to inflict on Nae would feel like once they started to heal.

Santana began to walk around the back of Pharaoh's car, and suddenly the street began to fill with hoodlums. She didn't know if Nae had called people ahead of time to tell them what was getting ready to go down or what, but she didn't care. She wasn't the one whose skin and behind were going to need a spatula to be scraped up off the street.

"Come on, Nae. You brought it, now bring it. Get out the car!" she dared her, banging on the trunk of the chickenhead-mobile Nae was in. "Come on! I'm inviting you to get that azz whooped."

"Man, I got twenty bones on Santana!" Some dude with jeans sagging off his butt and dirty, dusty boxers showing said, walking up to some guys while counting money.

"I'll match that," another agreed. "Shawty go to skool with my brutha, and she be mopping hallways with heads—boy's heads at dat!"

A boy with long, red dreadlocks countered. "Bwoy, please. Me tinks me put me money on de undah-dog. Dat der gal been hot for Pharaoh fa-evah. She not g'won to sekkle for less."

"Aw, Dread, speak American! Dis Hotlanta, not the islands. We don't know what you just said, but I'll take your money though!"

Santana stood in the middle of the street, waiting. She looked to her left, then her right, remembering Nae's scary behind wasn't alone. She was a true, bona fide scrapper, but she wasn't a fool. There, sitting next to the curb, was what she needed. A bottle.

"Come on, Nae!" she urged, walking over and picking

up the twenty-ounce glass weapon. She hit it against the concrete, breaking off enough to be able to hold it confidently. Its jagged edges were the perfect solution to a multi-girl fight.

Suddenly, out of nowhere, hands wrapped and held on to the back of her arms, pulling her back. Santana jerked her body and swung the broken bottle at her opponent. Pharaoh ducked and jumped back. "Santana stop! What you doing out here fighting in the skreet?" He reached for the bottle. "Gimme dat! You ain't goin' be out here fightin dat scallywag. For what, shawty?"

Santana snatched the bottle back. She didn't care how mad Pharaoh was or how violent his reputation, she wasn't giving up her weapon when she had so many enemies around.

"'Ey! Yo!" he boomed, walking up to the car Nae and her friends were in. "What's yo problem, Nae? What I tell you about trying my girl? Didn't I tell you if I ever catch you 'round her that I'd slap yo daddy so hard that *yo* head would split?"

From where she stood, Santana couldn't hear Nae, but she did see her cower.

"Get out the car!" Pharaoh yelled at Nae like she was his child. "Now! Or it ain't gone be me you havta to worry about, I'ma let Santana get you." He turned his head to a group of guys standing on a porch.

"'Ey, Gully! Come get my girl for me."

A lanky guy dressed in collegiate clothes bumbled down the porch steps and walked through the grassless yard.

"Okay, Pharaoh. Don't worry, I'll take care of her," the guy said, sounding like a textbook.

Santana looked at him, wondering where he'd come from. He was dressed too preppy and spoke too proper to be one of Pharaoh's boys.

"Don't touch me!" she hissed.

"So . . . Santana, how are you doing today? Rhetorical question. I apologize. Would you like to come in, maybe have a glass of water?"

Rhetorical? What the heck did rhetorical mean? she wondered, cringing at the too-proper way he spoke. To her he sounded like a computer, like the navigation system in her mother's car. No one spoke that way. She raised her eyebrows and flared her nostrils.

"Don't touch me or I'll slice this bottle across your face," she promised.

Gully put up his hands. "Okay. I promise not to touch you, but I'd like to help you calm down. I have some new equipment in the house that I'm constructing, and the processors are amazing. You should see the speed and memory—I'm talking way more megabytes and gigabytes known to man. I'm Gulliver, by the way, but Pharaoh calls me Gully."

"So?" Was he serious? she wondered, easing up on Pharaoh and Nae. She couldn't hear their conversation because of the human robot in front of her and the distance.

"What I tell you last week, Nae?" Pharaoh asked, pushing Nae toward the hooptie she'd come in, and forcing her to get inside.

Last week? Santana pushed Gully out of her way and

zoomed behind Pharaoh. "*Last week?* Did you just say you were talking to that trash *last* week? What the—why were you talking to her at *all*?"

Pharaoh shook his head. "Come on, Santana! Enough. Now you know I don't deal with her stankin' breath."

"Oh, he talks to me *all* the time. Last week and last night," Nae said, getting bold again from the safety of the car.

"Nae, why you lying?" Pharaoh banged on the roof of the car and reached to open the door. Before he could get a grip on it, the engine roared and the wheels spun, and the car sped off down the street.

Nae stuck her head out the window. "Want me to describe him naked to you, Santana?" She laughed like a banshee as the car disappeared in a literal cloud of stinky exhaust smoke.

Pharaoh turned and looked at Santana with disgust in his eyes. She knew better than to be fighting on the street, but she didn't care. Nae had left her no choice, and she wouldn't apologize for it. Plus, as far as she was concerned, Pharaoh—not she—had some explaining to do.

"Why were you talking to her?" Her eyes welled, and she gripped the neck of the broken bottle by her side.

Pharaoh looked from Santana's furious eyes to the bottle. "'Ey! Don't be ackin' like you wanna swing dat. I ain't Nae—you puts no fear in my heart, shawty. I run dis here block." He moved his eyes from her face and looked behind her. "'Ey, Gully! Take my girl home for me, bruh. I got bidness and don't want her in these skreets." He turned back to Santana. "I got something to do. But since you really wanna know, I saw that scallywag last week at the store, and she tried to get wit' ya boy, so I checked her. I'm yo man, shawty. Just yours." He bent down and planted a kiss on her lips, something he'd never done before in public. "I like dat you was gonna fight for yours, though. But you ain't godda fight for me, shawty. Fighting is my job. Your job is to tell me who you need knocked out." He winked.

Santana's anger caved, and she almost smiled.

"I'm ready, Pharaoh," Gully said, walking up to them.

Pharaoh peeled off a hundred-dollar bill from a thick stack of money. "Y'all take my car, and get something to eat. I'll get wit you later, shawty. I still got yo surprise."

Gully drove Pharaoh's car like an old man. His hands were placed on the wheel at the ten-o'clock and two-o'clock positions just as the driver's courses taught, and he'd done the speed limit—the exact speed limit, all the way to a restaurant Santana had never been to or heard of. *35mph, not a digit more or less. Sickening.*

Her stomach growled, and she sucked her teeth, looking away toward a group of people who sounded like they were talking in tongues. She didn't hear a word of English in the group.

"Our host should be here any minute," he said, apologetically. "Would you like me to see when they'll seat us?"

No, what I'd like you to do is learn how to speak and stop sounding like a robot, or stop talking to me, she thought, but instead shook her head no.

"Your name is very pretty, Santana. Reminds me of Carlos Santana. It's very telling, but I don't like to be one to assume. Does it bespeak your roots or nationality?"

Be-who?

The host came, beckoned them to follow him, and showed them to their table. Gully pulled out Santana's chair, then helped push her closer to the table. She thought his action was nice, but she'd never tell him. Holding out chairs wasn't in Pharaoh's makeup—people went out of their way for Pharaoh, not the other way around. But as long as he paid, Santana didn't care who held out her chair. She eyed Gully closely. He did one thing Pharaoh didn't, but he certainly wasn't Pharaoh.

He took her napkin from the table, snapped it opened, then placed it on her lap. *Okay. Two things.* What was he, a corner boy who spoke gentlemen's English and waited tables on the side? He sat down in his seat, and spread his napkin in his lap. *Okay. Three things.*

"Would you like me to order for you? Tell me what you like and—"

"I can order for myself. Who do you think you are, my daddy? Do I look three to you?"

Gully held up his hands, leaned back in his chair, then folded his arms in his lap. He seemed to be waiting.

Santana opened her menu, and to her surprise and embarrassment, the menu was written in a different language. Her eyebrows shot up.

"I'll just have the chicken."

They both laughed, and Santana's mood lightened.

"So you speak . . ." She looked at the menu again.

"Spanish, French, Italian, Portuguese, Patois, and, of course, English—except for slang. I'm not good with slang or dumbing down my vocabulary. I think, after a while, speaking badly affects a person's lexicon." Santana's eyebrows shot up. "Sorry, it affects a person's vocabulary."

Okay. Nine things, including a lexi-whatever.

They talked for a while, and Gulliver—what he preferred to be called, was a genuine nice guy. *Ten things.* No criminal record. *Eleven things.* No questionable business. *Twelve things.* And he was borderline genius, on his way to college a year and a half early to be an architectural engineer. *Thirteen, fourteen, and fifteen.* He volunteered at homeless shelters. *Sixteen.* Didn't wear clothes with the designer's name splashed all over the place. *Seventeen.* And built computers and databases, and designed video games for a living. *Eighteen, nineteen, twenty.*

"Why don't I know you? If Pharaoh let you use his car—left you alone with me, he has to trust you. So why don't I know you? I've never seen you before," she said, leaning forward on the table.

Gully smiled. "Of course you wouldn't know me. I grew up on the block, but I'm not a part of the block, Santana. I'm always away at school or on trips overseas—a survival mechanism, so to speak. I'm usually only home for the holidays. So unless you were at my house for Christmas or attending Easter service at my church, we wouldn't have met."

Santana nodded. That explained everything—especially the way he spoke and his politeness. The block hadn't ruined him or given him swagger.

"You know, Santana," he said, reaching into his pocket. He pulled out some money and slid a one-hundred-dollar bill to her and a card. "I really enjoy your company. As a gentleman, I can't let Pharaoh pay for dinner. You keep the money. This is my treat. And if you ever need help with school or need some work done on your computer, call me. That's my card."

Santana looked at him and smiled. *Twenty-one.* He was a perfect jackpot. Too bad he didn't have swagger. She'd bet a dollar to a dime, no Naes were lurking in his world.

5

DYNASTY

The bright green jelly shoes were sticking to the bottoms of her feet, and now had begun to make sucking noises when she walked. Swoosh. Smack. Flop. Swoosh. Smack. Flop. Dynasty made it to the barred door of the store, and pushed her way inside. Head-scarved women, dusty teenagers, and children with freshly greased hair and faces were inside, along with a few stray bums and corner boys. Her eyes roamed the counter, looking for Old Man Curtis, the owner. That's who she wanted to see. He was the only one who would help her.

"Get out!" an old-gruff voice boomed. "Whatcha loitering 'round here for?" Mr. Curtis appeared with a broom as ancient as he, and began sweeping dirt toward the bums and dusty teenage boys who'd come to his store hoping to make their own transactions. "Not in here! What I say about y'all trying to sell that poison in my store? Get out! And I ain't gonna call no police neither. I'm the law 'round here. So get, before I go get Lucy."

Dynasty smiled as the unwelcomed riffraff left the store. No one wanted Mr. Curtis to get Lucy, his sawed-off shotgun. He'd been known to pull her out in the past, and use her too.

"Afternoon, Mr. Curtis."

He held up his finger to quiet her, then waited for the store to clear. One lone boy got cocky, refusing to move from the potato-chip rack.

"All right, young'un, you done asked for it." Mr. Curtis bobbled as fast as he could toward the counter, looking like he was ready to jump into double-Dutch ropes. One of his legs was significantly shorter than the other, so he rocked side to side when he walked. Reaching behind the counter, he grabbed his precious Lucy. The boy was gone before he could turn around. "These fools 'round here ain't got the sense God gave 'em! Lawd ha-mercy." He looked at Dynasty, and flashed her a toothless smile. "Now what'chu want, lil gal?"

Dynasty's stare hit the floor. She'd had to come to Mr. Curtis for help before, and it never got easier. "Is there anything I can do for you around here?"

"I done told you I can't hire you. You ain't old enough, and you doggone sure ain't big enough. Folks see you in here and they gone think they can get away with murder. Child, I got thoughts bigger than you; you ain't big as a fly wing, so how you gonna stop these thieves and riffraff from loitering? Huh?" His voice was rough, but his eyes were warm.

The bell above the door rang, signaling someone had entered the store.

"Come on, child. Speak!" Mr. Curtis urged. "I ain't gots all day."

Dynasty looked up into his eyes with tears in her own. "Mr. Curtis, I know you can't hire me, but I only need to make a few dollars. Today. If I don't make money—only ten dollars—I can't go home."

Mr. Curtis exhaled. "It's your auntie again, huh? I swear that's the craziest loon I've ever seen. What she do to you this time? Beat ya?"

"Can I get my lotto tickets up in here, please? I need to play my numbers! Today is the day, Curtis! I'm gonna hit big. Come on. . . . You can talk to that hungry-looking child later," said some man with too-short overalls, rolled-down socks, and a cigarette butt hanging from the side of his mouth.

"Shut up, Red! I'm coming." Mr. Curtis looked at Dynasty. "Wait here." He rocked his way toward the back of the register.

"I only need to make ten dollars!" yelled Dynasty. "I can sweep, break down boxes, stock shelves . . . anything."

"Does anything include knowing your way around, miss?" a raspy voice with clipped words asked from behind in what sounded like an English accent.

"Of course," Dynasty answered before she turned and saw who the voice belonged to. As long as she was safe, she didn't care. Ten dollars was ten dollars and a way to keep a roof over her head and Aunt Maybelline's foot from connecting with her butt.

"Word?"

Word? What did that mean? Dynasty wondered. She had never heard that expression before, and knew that the person with the raspy voice wasn't from her housing project. She turned around and locked eyes with the stranger. She was right. There was no way on heaven or earth that they came from the same place. He was almost as tall as Rufus, Oreo-cookie chocolate, with the longest eyelashes she'd ever seen, and a long jagged scar on the right side of his face. His features were very pronounced, and said his ethnic roots ran deep. He was stately, standing erect as if no one or nothing could sway him. He was sure. If she had to sum him up in one word, it'd be supreme. She guessed he had to be at least sixteen or seventeen.

He pulled a thick wad of money from his pocket, and began peeling off ones from the stack. "Ten. Right, miss?"

Suddenly Dynasty felt insecure. She looked at his fresh clothes. Jeans that looked like they cost lots of money. Shirt that said the same. Prada sneakers that she'd never seen anyone around her way wear, so she knew they were the real deal. Then she glanced down at her own tangerine, aqua, white, and yellow halter top, orange booty shorts, and fluorescent green jelly shoes, and remembered the ragged purple scarf tied on her head. She shook her head. "I'm sorry, I can't. I don't know you. Plus, I have to go home and study semantics, morphology, and etymology," she said, turning away from him. She loved his accent, look, the way he called her miss, but she was from the projects, and project girls knew better than to go off with strangers, because most times you never came back.

"Lil gal, if your crazy auntie don't let you back in today or she beat you, you come back here tomorrow. I'll see what I can do for you," Mr. Curtis called out from behind the counter.

Tomorrow? I could be dead by then. Dynasty pushed open the door, then slid her way back out into the broiling heat. Her feet slapped against the broken blacktop as she made her way through the parking lot and down the block. She had to figure out something to tell Aunt Maybelline, or risk sleeping on the front steps again.

"Shuckey duckey, quack, quack. Unlucky, hungry-looking, and burnt black. What's going on Die Nasty?" Rufus teased, bounding his hundreds of pounds toward the store, with sweat pouring from his pores, streaking down his forehead, and gathering in the dark folds of his neck.

Dynasty stopped, put her hands on her nonexistent hips, and looked him square in the eyes. "Not today, Dufus! Oops, I mean, Rufus!" She waited for him to reach her, then walked by him. With the nonsense she had to go home to, she didn't have time for Rufus's buffoonery.

Rufus pivoted, then began walking behind her. "You know what, Die Nasty Young? You too skinny, and you think you too smart and good for people. I only came to help you carry your beer and cigarettes . . . since you *thirteen*. With your lying self, telling your crazy auntie that."

Her eyes widened. Rufus could've only gotten that information from one person. "And you know what, troglodyte? You look like you stink. Go somewhere."

"And you look like you're about five minutes from being homeless! That's what your dear Aunt Maybelline's outside telling everybody—if you don't have her beer and cigarettes . . . and I don't see no Bud or Newports."

Dynasty swallowed the unkind remark she had for Rufus and kept walking. She couldn't believe Aunt May-belline was outside telling everyone what Rufus just told her. But, then again, she could. It wasn't as if this was the first time Aunt Maybelline was putting their business on the street. Every time she'd forgotten or refused to take her medication, she'd put on a show, and Dynasty would be the laughing stock of the projects. She wished her mother would get off drugs and her brother would come home from jail, but she knew the likelihood of either wasn't high.

"Whatchu thinking about, Dynasty? Lipstick and King? Well, your aunt said King ain't coming home from prison this week like you lied and said. So maybe Lip-stick will swirl your way and save you." He laughed a big fat jolly laugh.

Dynasty looked back, cut her eyes at Rufus, and snatched Aunt Maybelline's bright green jelly shoe off her foot in one swoop. It left her small hand, spinning like a torpedo, and bounced off of Rufus's forehead.

"Don't talk about my momma, Rufus. And you can listen to Aunt Maybelline about King if you want. I told you he's coming home *this* week, didn't I? So when he comes for you, you better be ready." The wind gusted, blowing specks of dirt in her face. She dabbed her tearing eyes.

"Ouch. That's why your brother's named after a dog. Aunt Maybelline said that too. I had a dog named King once. A pit bull."

A black car with shiny silver rims pulled alongside her, on the wrong side of the street. The door opened, and the guy from the store got out.

"Yo son!" he barked on Rufus with his clipped English accent. "Why you bothering her for? She like one-fourth your size, kid. What's the deal with that?"

"Come on, City, man. We was just playing. We've been friends forever, that's just how we conversate. Ask her." Rufus said.

Rufus knew him? She wondered how that was possible, when she didn't.

"Yo, what I tell you about all that playing, son? Look at what you've done to her—she's in tears over here." He shook his head in disgust. "Pardon me, miss. You a'ight?"

Dynasty looked at the guy from the store with new eyes. He was as supreme as she'd thought, and his Oreo-cookie-brown complexion was even more beautiful in the sunlight. Compared to Rufus sweating like a stuck hog, City hadn't a trace of perspiration.

"I'm okay. I don't pay Rufus any attention; he's a bit . . . well, different. But he's my friend—on most days."

"You the one who different, Dynasty! That's why your aunt gonna kicks you out if you don't have her beer and cigarettes! About the ten dollars. City, you heard about her, right? The crazy lady that's loony."

"Stop talking in fragments, Rufus. And make your subjects and verbs agree. And by the way, it's *you're* and *who's*, not you and that's. Who is for a person, that is for a thing."

The guy posted up. He moved his feet until they were shoulder width apart, and clasped hands in front of him. He turned only his face, and glared at Rufus. "Yo son, for real, though. I'm not going to tell you any more—lay off, kid. That's my word." He turned back to Dynasty. "That's your real name, miss? Dynasty?"

She nodded, stopping herself from smiling. With only a few sentences the guy had managed to make Rufus shut up.

"I like that. That's what I'm building—a dynasty. They call me City because I'm from up north. Brooklyn, USA. So now that I know why you need ten dollars, you sure you don't want to show me where I need to go? I can't get Meka—that's my people—to show me, she's too busy working. And if you can do it, I can pay you up front, that way your aunt or whoever will fall back. And beer and cigarettes aren't a problem either, that's an easy fix." He held up his hands in surrender. "You can trust me, Dynasty. You can ask Rufus or Pork Chop. Even Old Man Curtis can vouch for me. I'm on the up and up."

So his accent wasn't English. City was from the city, and now she could tell. That's where his clipped words, almost one-hundred-percent-proper enunciation, authentic Prada sneakers, and sure demeanor came from. Dynasty looked at Rufus, and he nodded his head.

"Pork Chop's his granddaddy."

Dynasty raised her eyebrows, then cupped her hands over them. The sun was high in the sky and burning too bright to see without shade. "And you're going to give me the money up front?"

He reached into his pocket and handed it to her.

"And take me home so I can change?"

"With pleasure."

Dynasty nodded, not sure if City was being smart-alecky or not about her multi-Crayola-colored outfit. But she didn't care; if he was Pork Chop's grandson, she felt as if she could trust him, plus she needed his ten dollars more than ever. "Okay. Where do you have to go?" she asked, walking toward his car.

City jogged slightly in front of her, then opened the passenger door. "On Peach something. May be Peachtree."

She got inside the car, welcoming the clean scent and cool air. "Peach or Peachtree?" She laughed. "That could mean one of a hundred different streets here. It could take all day," she warned him.

City rounded the car, then hopped in on the driver's side. "Word? I'm good with that. . . . I like being in the company of pretty girls. First, answer something for me, Dynasty? I consider myself to be a pretty smart dude, and you stumped me earlier, and it's been bothering me ever since. What does that morph, eta . . . you know what I'm talking about—the stuff you study. What does all that mean?"

"Oh you mean morphology, semantics, and etymology. They're studies of words. Respectively, word structure and form, words and language forms, and word origins."

City whistled. "Beautiful *and* smart? Today is going to be a great day, Dynasty. No, this week is going to be a good week. I promise you that."

Dynasty blushed. No one had ever called her beautiful or smart, or promised her a good day or week. She knew there was something she liked about City.

6

PATIENCE

The dude who Silky said was hers was beautiful. Clear skin and well groomed, his hair looked like he'd just left the barbershop. Diamonds, the size of plump raisins, gleamed from both his ears, almost blinding her. Winking, he licked his lips, then spread his mouth into a crooked smile. His white teeth clashed against the dimness of the truck and the gold grills on his homeboys' teeth.

Mmm. She inhaled the boy's beauty when Silky moved away from him and settled herself on the guy's lap next to him. Patience blinked slowly and gulped even slower. She was in serious trouble. Trouble because as much as she knew she shouldn't be in the truck, and as much of a rage as the good Bishop Blackman would be in if he ever found out, she didn't care. *Sorry, Bishop.* The caramel-dipped guy who sat across from her with flawless skin and a thin line of hair over his yummy lips made her forget the most important thing she'd been taught—respect her parents. He'd moved her with only a smile.

"S'up, lil momma?" he asked, sitting across from her, handing her a bottle of something that looked like liquid amber.

Her knees were inches away from his long legs, but her heart was already in his hands. Patience shrugged and inched back into the seat. That was her way of declining his offer.

"What's the matter? Something holding your tongue?"

The three other boys laughed.

"Yeah, homeboy. You holding it. You know they always freeze when you speak," the guy sitting next to her said.

Why and who were *they*? she wondered, looking from the guys to Silky and sliding farther over from the boy next to her. Silky smiled and hunched her shoulders.

"So . . . are you like a backup dancer for Silky's mom or something?" Patience asked Pretty Boy, noticing that his arms were very toned. Pretty Boy had to be his name or at least his nickname. He was too beautiful to be called anything else.

Pretty Boy raised his brows and froze for half a second. His expression registered shock. He shook his head and grinned again, blinding her with that ultra-white crooked smile.

The other three boys were silent, while two of them looked from Patience to Pretty Boy to Silky, then began Ping-Ponging their eyes back and forth between the three again.

"Hmm," the one with Silky on his lap growled, then

wrapped his arms around Silky's middle. To Patience he sounded like a rottweiler and looked like one trying to claim her best friend as his territory.

"I told you!" Silky cheesed, comfortably leaning back into the boy. "This here is my girl. I. Know. Her. What I say? I told you!"

Patience looked sideways at Silky. She knew her best friend meant her no harm, but she was starting to not appreciate being the only one who seemed not to know what was going on.

"Told them what?"

Pretty Boy reached over and grabbed her knee. "You a good girl. That's the verdict. Huh, lil momma?"

Patience nodded, then shrugged. She realized he'd barely moved forward to touch her. He had to be tall. "I guess."

"What's the last movie you went to?" His stare made her wiggle. No one had ever made her feel so uncomfortable before, not like this, and it was baffling her. The feelings he'd caused her moved through her like waves. Good ones that tickled and excited her all at once, and she wanted to laugh out loud but didn't want to make herself look like a kid.

She shook her head.

"Last video game you played or bought?" the boy on the other side of him asked.

She rotated her head no again.

"Last concert?" Silky quizzed with a knowing look and smile that said she'd already told them all of Patience's lack of worldly culture.

Patience cut her eyes. Silky knew the answer.

"You know."

Silky shook her head, then sang, "I've been gone two months. . . . Anything could've changed."

"Gospel Fest," Patience whispered, feeling like a fool on display.

"Favorite TV show . . ."

Patience held up her hand, signaling she was done being interrogated. "I don't go to movies, play video games, watch cable TV, or go to real concerts. I don't do anything. Okay?" she snapped, embarrassed.

Pretty Boy smiled. "No need to be mad, lil momma. I think it's wonderful. We're celebrating you, not making fun of you. 'Least I'm not. . . ."

She looked over at him, then blinked away quickly. He was so fine she couldn't connect her eyes with his because she was sure her feelings were obvious. Bishop Blackman's warning bounced through her head. *Boys aren't any good. Any! All they want is one thing. One! They take the milk and leave the cow, and they don't even feed it first. Don't feed it. Don't love it. Don't care if it cries.*

The SUV jerked to a stop. "Sorry, sir," the driver's voice came through the speakers, bringing Patience's attention to another thing she'd missed. The SUV had a black glass partition between the front and the back, which someone had rolled down a couple of inches.

She sat for a second watching all the guys except Pretty Boy collect bottles of alcohol, cell phones, iPods, and bags of fast food and doughnuts. Silky's growler hopped out of the SUV first, followed by Silky and the boy who sat next to Patience. The guy who sat on the other side of Pretty Boy climbed out of the other door, then offered her his hand to help her out of the vehicle.

"Go 'head, lil momma. My homeboy Big Dude don't bite—he just look like he do."

It was then that Patience realized she'd been staring at the guy's hand like he had leprosy. "Sorry and thank you," she said, climbing out with his assistance, then staring at him. Big Dude, if that was in fact his name, was big. Statue of Liberty huge.

He smiled and reminded her of an overstuffed, giant-sized teddy bear like the one she'd won at Six Flags. He nodded. "Yuh, they call me Big Dude. And no, thank you." He turned his attention to Pretty Boy. " 'Bout time we got somebody 'round here with manners."

"Dat's what I'm talum'bout," Pretty Boy said, emerging from the vehicle, speaking another language and standing about six feet tall.

"Huh?" Patience accidentally wrinkled her nose, trying to figure out what language he was speaking.

"Ah, partna, shawty ain't skreet. Godda clean 'tup," Big Dude said to Pretty Boy, slamming the door shut behind him and shadowing him like a redwood tree.

"Patience, he said that's what he's talking about, and Big Dude said you're not from the streets, that he should talk proper so you understand, that he should clean up his words," Silky interpreted, rounding the back of the SUV.

Patience formed her lips into a circle, but before she could respond "oh" her eyes flashed to her right and she noticed they were in the VIP valet at Phipps Plaza, the upscale mall in Buckhead. People stood around in amazement, staring at them and taking pictures with cell phones and cameras. She bucked her eyes a little, not understanding the people's greenness. Just because they were in VIP and hopping out of a stretch luxury SUV didn't mean they were superstars, though being next to Pretty Boy made her feel like one.

He grabbed her hand, lacing his fingers through hers. "Come on, my little good girl," he said and took a step toward the entrance. Some girls rushed toward them, and Pretty Boy pulled her close to him. "They got us, lil momma." He nodded his head toward Big Dude and the other guys. "No need to get nervous; you might wanna get used to it."

Big Dude and Growler became walls of steel right before her eyes. They slid in front of her and Pretty Boy, blocking the girls. The other guy quickened his pace until he was in front of them, making the crowd part like the Red Sea Bishop Blackman loved to preach about when talking about making a way out of no way.

Patience shot Silky a look. Silky just pursed her lips, rolled her eyes toward the girls, and mouthed "haters" while she walked beside Growler. They both laughed. *People can be so silly because of limousines and VIP sections,* Patience thought, gripping Pretty Boy's hand as they walked through the mall.

"OMG," some young girl said, walking past them.

"What it was, cuz?" a boy with his pants hanging off his butt asked, walking by them.

"Hey . . . is that? Are you . . . ?" Somebody's mother asked, then shook her head and began talking on her cell phone. "Girl, that's not him."

Out of nowhere a girl squealed and jumped up and down.

Patience shook her head. She'd been in Phipps Plaza more times than she could count, and she'd never encountered such weirdness. She felt a slight elbow in her ribs. She looked at it, then up at whom it belonged to. Pretty Boy was smiling at her with his eyes.

"This crazy, right? We just came to get some shoes, that's all."

"It's different," she said. "They all act like . . ." A moment of realization hit her then, and she looked at the guy walking in front of them. She had seen people act like this before. There were times she'd been out with Bishop and people would come up to them acting starstruck, blinded by his position and his notoriety.

"Like what?" Pretty Boy prodded.

Patience eyed his friend a little bit more, saw how laid back he was, and decided she'd been wrong. She didn't want to seem any more foolish than she'd felt in the truck. "I don't know. . . ." Her words drifted off when she smelled caramel. She'd become so thirsty her feet stopped moving, and so did everyone else's. The aroma reminded her of Pretty Boy's complexion and the iced caramel Macchiato she suddenly craved.

"Oww. I know you smell that!" Silky sang, tilting her head toward Patience, and unhooking her arm from the growler. "Right back, baby. Right back. The caramel's calling."

Patience looked at Pretty Boy. "You mind?"

He shook his head and stuck his hand in his pocket.

Patience walked off toward the coffee stand in the middle of the mall for the expensive drink, then looked over her shoulder. He was watching her. It seemed they all were.

"So . . . whatcha think. He's fine, huh?" Silky quizzed before Patience finished ordering.

All Patience could do was nod. "Later," she whispered. "Okay?"

Silky looked over her shoulder. "Ill. They staring. He's staring at you. Lucky. Lucky. Lucky."

"Patience? Cuz is that you?"

Patience turned, and a smile parted her lips. "Meka? Hey cousin! What are you doing here?"

"What it was, cuz?" Meka walked up and greeted her, then nodded at Silky. She held up department store bags. "Shopping—my way, as usual. What's up with you? I can't believe The Good Reverend Doctor let you out," she said, laughing. "But you're good, right?"

Patience nodded. "I'm great. You want to come hang with me and Silky?"

Meka looked over her shoulder, then shook her head. "Nah. Security's too beefed up around here. It's in and out for me. Maybe we can get up later. I godda go find my girl, Santana. It's time for us to be out!" She looked around again. "Yep. Y'all be safe. Call me if you need me."

Patience nodded, smiling as her cousin disappeared. She grabbed the drinks and walked over to the sugar and milk station. She put two sugars in each, stirred, and closed them, then walked back over to Pretty Boy. "Here. I made yours like I made mine. Hope you don't mind. I'm sorry, I should've asked you what you wanted."

Pretty Boy bit his bottom lip, shot a quick glance at each of his friends, nodded, and took the specialty iced coffee. He smiled at Patience, then sipped from the straw.

"Thanks, lil momma."

His friends were oohing and ahhing, making street-boy catcalls, which amounted to a bunch of "Yeahs" and "That's what's ups."

"What I say? I told y'all!" Silky sang again.

"You didn't buy me one," the growler growled.

Pretty Boy took Patience's free hand in his. "Come with me," he said, pulling her away from the crowd. He stopped walking when they were by Tiffany & Co., one of her mother's favorite jewelry stores. "I really appreciate the coffee, and I know we don't know each other that well, but I'm also here because it's my mom's birthday." He shrugged. "But I'm a lil short on cash, and it's Sunday so the bank's closed. . . ." His eyes were warm and trusting, and had filled with love when he mentioned his mother.

Patience nodded. She handed him her drink, reached in her purse, and pulled out her wallet.

"What are you doing?" he asked.

She opened her wallet, took out a bill, and handed it to him. "I have fifty dollars from working at the church—"

Pretty Boy held up his hands, both filled with a caramel macchiato in a venti cup. "Hold up. Hold up. You're going to give me money?"

Patience looked up, saw how shocked he was. She was

sure he'd said he was short on buying his mother a gift. "You said you're a little short, right?"

He stepped back, looked her up and down, then tilted his head. "When do I godda pay you back?"

Patience smiled. One thing her parents taught her that she hadn't forgotten today was don't lend, give. Even that was in The Good Book. Never a lender or a borrower be. She shrugged because she didn't know what else to do.

"Never. It's for your mother's gift."

He took the money she handed him, closed his eyes for seconds, then looked at her. He handed her a cup, whipped out his cell phone, and began texting. Suddenly, his friends and Silky were walking up to them.

"Stay right here. Okay, lil momma," he said, handing her his cup. He tilted his head toward Tiffany & Co. and his boys followed him inside.

"What did you do?" Silky asked.

"Nothing. I gave him some money to help buy his mother a birthday present."

Silky's head almost came off, she'd turned it so fast. "You what? What?"

Patience repeated herself.

Silky threw one hand on her hip and leaned into it. "He didn't ask you for no—"

"No! He didn't ask for anything. He just kind of mentioned he was short on the money he needed because today's Sunday and the bank's closed."

Silky's eyebrows shot toward the heavens.

Like a vampire, Pretty Boy and two of his friends appeared out of nowhere. "Come on, lil momma," he said, taking his cup from her and lacing his fingers through hers again. He looked at her softly from the corner of his eye, then shook his head in what she assumed to be disbelief.

In seconds, they'd walked into one department store, and made an immediate right into Louis Vuitton, which was housed in a room all its own. And Patience was in heaven. She loved bags. All bags. Ones with names and others without.

"That's hot right there," Pretty Boy said, pointing to one of the newest ones.

Patience nodded. "It is, but that one—" She pointed to a different one. "I don't know, it may be nicer. If I was your mother, I'd want that one because it's more subtle."

Pretty Boy looked at her and smiled. "Subtle? I like that." He turned his attention to an employee, pointed at the bag he'd picked out, then the one Patience had chosen. "We'll take both, and we'll need shoes and sunglasses to match."

"Okay. And what size would you like?"

Pretty Boy looked at Patience. "Tell him your size, lil momma."

Patience pointed at her chest. "My size?"

"Excuse me?" a little girl no more than ten walked up to them, tapping Pretty Boy on his arm.

They both turned and looked at her.

"I'm sorry to bother you, but can I please have your autograph and a picture?"

Patience looked at the little girl, then at Pretty Boy.

"Me too, if you don't mind, sir," the salesman asked.

Patience froze. "I'm sorry. . . . What's your name?" she finally asked him.

"OMG," the little girl said. "What tree have you been living in?"

The salesman tilted his head. "Honey, he's only the biggest rapper on the planet, and he's buying you shoes and bags and sunglasses. Are you kidding me?"

Pretty Boy just nodded.

7

DYNASTY

Dynasty sat under the sorry excuse for a tree, cradling her prized dictionary in her lap, studying her words of the week. "Foment..." The sun crept into her eyes, making her shift her position on the flimsy piece of cardboard that separated her from the ground. The red clay was too dry to properly nourish the tree, and the sparse leaves had all but disappeared, allowing light to glare on the pages. But it would have to do; Aunt Maybelline was having a grown-up party, complete with Al Green albums blasting from the old-school record player, cigarette smoke, and loud liquored-up adults who turned up their volume more and more with each drink, so there was nowhere for her to study in her tenement. But she had to get her words in for the week. She had a date—yes, a date—but she couldn't let that deter her from her mission: to get out of the PJs and into an Ivy League college.

"*Foment*. Foh-mehnt. Verb. To incite or arouse . . . like agitate. Used in a sentence: The students tried to *foment* a food fight in the cafeteria with the class president because he was *perfidious*, and had sided against the school offering soda. *Perfidious*. Puhr-*fih*-dee-uhs. Adjective. Willing to betray one's trust . . . like disloyal." She closed the dictionary.

Leaning to one side, she looked over at her nonexistent butt, making sure she hadn't gotten her one pair of good pants dirty. She'd taken the ten dollars City had given her to the local under-twenty dollars store and bought them after he'd made sure someone had bought Aunt Maybelline's beer and cigarettes. A car engine roared, pulling her attention. City was due to pick her up at any moment, and she wouldn't dare make him wait. He was her temporary escape from the projects and Aunt Maybelline. Rufus too. *Oh, boy,* she thought, seeing him walk her way. She quickly reopened the dictionary and buried her attention back into the book.

The human cloud loomed over her now, shading her and the dictionary from the sun. She pretended she didn't know he was there, and ignored his heavy breathing and the shuffling of the biggest feet she'd ever seen. He'd worn a size fourteen last year, so he had to be at least a fifteen or better now. Rufus plopped down next to her, his heaviness causing a thin film of dirt to jump and hover. He'd reminded her of Pig-Pen, the Charlie Brown character who always had a puff of dirt around him. But she decided against saying so and swallowed her words. It was hard not to tell him how clumsy and rude he was for interrupting her because he deserved it, and she knew he wanted her to, just so he'd have some fuel to start an argument. But she ignored him. He just wasn't worth her time, and as much as he got on her nerves, she knew deep down that he wasn't so bad. Not all the time. He just wanted attention.

He picked up a stick from the ground, started drawing figures in the dirt, and waited for her to acknowledge him. "So Die Nasty, whatchu reading? That dumb dictionary that you think gonna get you out of here?" He laughed.

Dynasty cut her eyes at Rufus, then slammed shut her dictionary. "See that's your problem, Rufus. This is why you don't have any friends, besides me, and on most days you push me away with your attitude. You always have to start trouble for no reason." She got up from the ground, dusted her behind, and put the book under her arm. She didn't leave though, because where would she go? She'd already been chased out of the house to make room for Aunt Maybelline's old-biddy friends and the ever-present Pork Chop, who she was starting to suspect was her aunt's boyfriend. "Why don't you go somewhere, Rufus? I just want to study." She put her hand on her hip bone, glaring at him.

Rufus looked up, still swirling the stick around in the red dirt. He shrugged. "Why don't you? Why don't you go find J.R. and see if he'll give you the ten dollars he took? I heard you paid him to kiss you, and he didn't. I don't see you all up in his face—you too ashamed. Huh? He kissed you, ripped you, and ditched you, Die Nasty. I know you was with him, so you might as well admit it. You let him feel on you . . . didn't you?"

She shook her head, then noticed a shiny black car with sparkling rims rolling in the parking lot. A smile spread on her face, and any bad feeling Rufus had caused disappeared. Then she noticed something else, and her grin faded. City and J.R. were riding together.

Rufus noticed too, then fell back laughing. "Wow! I see both of your men—oops, I meant both of the ones you want and can't have—are together! I would love to know what they're talking about. Die Nasty did this to me. Well, she let me do that to her in the back of the building," he mused, making up his lies as he went along. "They don't want you, like I do. They just gonna use you up."

She ignored Rufus, and stood there in semi-amazement and full-fledged disappointment. She couldn't believe City was with J.R. The other day when she'd shown him around she'd confided in him, told him about her unlucky life and how she planned to snag a full scholarship to escape, and told him that J.R. had taken off with her aunt's money, which is why she couldn't go home. He'd listened intently, pep-talking her through it all, then admitted to knowing who J.R. was, and called him a punk. And now they were together? She didn't get it.

Rufus rolled over on his side, laughing and holding his belly. She looked back at him and wondered when he was going to be fitted with a bra. He was so big that his breasts were bigger than hers.

The car pulled up, and both doors opened. City stepped out first. He was a vision in contrast to the dusty surroundings. Rocking all white and some sort of shoes she'd never seen, but guessed were pricey, he adjusted the

fitted hat on his head, then wiped nonexistent perspiration from his brow. His skin, even before he'd "dried" it,
was dry and smooth as usual. Dynasty wondered if he'd
ever broken a sweat. He nodded at her, then leaned on
the car, looking toward the passenger side. J.R. emerged
as if on cue. He wasn't as rowdy, secure, or loud as he
usually was. In fact, she noticed, he was quiet. Without
making eye contact with her, he strutted over to her,
reached in his pocket, and pulled out a ten-dollar bill,
then handed it to her.

"Sorry," he mumbled.

City cleared his throat.

J.R. reached back in his pocket again, retrieving more
money. He handed her a twenty. "Interest . . ."

City cleared his throat again. "Yo, son! Don't forget
the rest."

J.R. looked up, focusing on the tree limbs. "Rufus, I
lied. I didn't hit her."

Rufus struggled, but managed to get up. "Huh?"

J.R. put his hands in his pockets. "I said, me and Dynasty didn't cut." He turned around to City. "We good
now? Can I go?"

City threw up his hands and shrugged. "I don't know,
kid. Something else that I don't know about that you
need to fix? You stole from her. Lied on her. What else?"
He waved his hand. "Yo son, disappear." He looked at
Rufus, and gave him a head nod, then turned to Dynasty.
"Are you ready for your life to change, Dynasty?"

Rufus snapped his fingers. "Yo, City! Them Louis boat
shoes? 'Ey, Jigga rapped about those. They must've cost a
grip."

City nodded, then went to hold open the passenger door for Dynasty as she took the first step of her new journey.

City was swift, she discovered. He talked fast and made major moves, had all the energy and pizzazz she'd heard New Yorkers had.

"Pay attention to the hustle, Dynasty. All of them aren't bad. But in this world there are two ways to live. You either make it happen, or watch it happen. I make things happen and, now, so do you because you're a part of my team. And we all have to eat. Nah'mean?" he'd said, before they'd entered the modern library that she'd never been to. In five minutes, with no ID of her own, City had dropped game on some unsuspecting teen girl behind the customer-service desk, and secured Dynasty a library card. He'd sat back with the proud face of a father while she perused the shelves, stacking book on top of book, eager to lose herself between the pages.

"Slow down, Dynasty. You can come back whenever."

She discovered why he'd slowed her down in the library when they'd made their next stop. He'd cruised up GA 400 highway to the prestigious town of Alpharetta, exited on 8, then turned right and navigated to North Point Parkway, where he made a sharp left and cruised to a parking lot. They passed a movie theater and parked in front of a Starbucks. Again, he rounded the car and opened her door. Stepping out, she looked at the sign, the tables outside, and the people sitting there drinking coffee while holding conversations and tapping away on their laptops.

"Thirsty?" she asked him, following him to the entrance.

He opened the door for her, then entered behind her. "Follow me," he said, then walked past the counter, the patrons standing in line for the caffeinated fixes, and the glass enclosure that housed brownies, Rice Krispies treats, and different kinds of cakes and muffins.

Dynasty drew her eyebrows together. If they weren't here to get coffee or a treat, what was the point in coming to Starbucks? In only three more steps, she had her answer. Through the coffee shop was an opening. A welcoming room full of wonderment, awe, and words. A bookstore. A huge chain store with rows and rows of books that tickled her mind and made her mouth water. Never mind the sweets that were housed in the glass enclosure only ten steps behind. Here were the real treats that could help her get where she wanted to be. Yes, they'd gone to the library, and she'd appreciated that. But those books she'd have to return. These books could belong to her.

City fished in his pocket and pulled out a plastic card. He handed it to her. "Since you like dictionaries so much, I was thinking you could get a new, updated one, and one of the books you mentioned the other day while we were riding."

Her eyes were stretched wide, and she was sure her smile was the same. She couldn't remember what book she'd told him about, but she could use the dictionary. An unabridged one with the complete list of current English words was something she'd wanted for a long time. She just hoped the card had enough money on it.

"There's about ninety dollars left on the card," said City.

Before she knew it, she'd stood on tiptoe and had her arms wrapped around him. She kissed him on his cheek. "Thank you so much, City. Because of you and all you've done for me today, I may have a chance of getting into my dream school, Winchester Hills Prep." Her eyes teared. No one had ever done something so fantastic for her before. Then a thought occurred, and she tried to make it disappear, but it wouldn't. The project girl instincts she'd tried to hone since middle school said there might be a catch. What did he want in return? She'd only shown him around, and he'd paid her for that, so why wouldn't he want some sort of payment now? She handed him back the card. "I can't take this—I don't have anything to offer you for it."

City pushed it back at her. "You have a lot to offer, Dynasty." He put his finger to her temple. "This. Your brain and what you want to do in life is payment enough . . . and maybe showing me around from time to time. I get lost in this country place. I'm from the city. I need a grid to maneuver—streets in numerical order." He smiled. "Now get your dictionary and . . . oh, that's right, the book to help you get into college."

"The SAT book."

"Yeah, that book. Then one more surprise."

North Point Mall was located across the street and up the block from the bookstore. Dynasty sat back in her seat, flipping through the new dictionary. She guessed it had to weigh close to ten pounds, and she couldn't wait to devour the words until her mind felt just as heavy. The car came to a stop, and she looked up. They were parked in front of the food court entrance, and she could see a merry-go-round spinning through the glass.

"She should be here in just a second," said City, as he scrolled through his cell phone, then looked out the driver's window.

Who is *she?* Dynasty wondered, but not for long.

A bump caused her to jump and look behind her. A pretty girl with short hair styled to perfection knocked on the trunk, and walked to City's door. Another beautiful girl with an expertly spiked Mohawk trailed behind her. Both had huge Gucci bags and were dressed to the hilt. City opened his door, then asked Dynasty to get out.

"Meka, baby!" he said to the girl with the short hair. "Whatcha got for me?"

Meka smiled. "Whatever you need . . . and if not today, then later. Just let me know the size, and you know I got you. Oh," she said turning to the girl with the Mohawk, "this is my BFF, Santana. Whatever I don't have, she does."

City nodded. "Family business? You know I like that. Speaking of family—" He nodded his head toward the other side of the car where Dynasty stood. "This here is my fam, Dynasty. I need some things for her—a lot, so look out on the price. Dynasty, this is my people, Meka." He tilted his head, then winked at Dynasty. "Forgot to tell you, we got a barbecue to go to. There's some people you need to meet."

"We'll be there, too," Meka said. "You know Santana's boo is throwing it."

8

SANTANA

Santana's jaw hung to the floor. She stood in her bedroom doorway, or what she'd thought was her doorway—what used to be hers—and bit her tongue. She wanted to scream, curse, or slap someone, but she couldn't. She shook her head. Every single thing that had belonged to her was missing. Bed. Flat-screen TV. Dresser. Wardrobe large enough for two teenagers. Even the pretty, girly-pink paint that had once colored her walls—all gone. "What in the heh—"

"You betta not cuss in my house," her mother said, walking around her into the room. She carried something large, black, and flat with a cord dangling.

"Mom—"

"Shhp." Her mother hushed her. "What I tell you about that? We're only fifteen years apart." She set down the computer monitor on an oversized desk that Santana had never seen. It still had bubble wrap on it, a telltale sign of it being new and just delivered. Fixing her hair, her mother stepped in front of the mirrored closet door and admired her youthful beauty. "Please. We look like sisters, so I can't be Mom, Momma, Mother, any M word. Do I look like one?"

Santana shook her head more in disgust than in answer. "What happened to my stuff? Where's my bedroom? Where am I supposed to sleep?" Her hands were on her hips and her upper lip was curled in a snarl. She knew she was being disrespectful, but her mother wanted to be treated like a sister, so Santana always did just that. She saved her respect for her grandmother.

"First, let's be clear." She turned to Santana, her scowl matching that on the face of the younger version of her. "Your room, sister girl, is where I say it is. You don't pay rent so you don't get to choose. This here room now belongs to Craig. It's his office—my surprise to him. You think he'll like it?" A smile crept on her face.

Santana couldn't believe her mother. Here she had taken her room away, and was acting like it was no big deal. And it wasn't. Not to her mother, anyway. She'd always chosen men over Santana. "Why does he get my room?"

"Craig gets your room because *he* pays rent." She busied herself, positioning the monitor, desk, and massive office chair. "Your new sleeping quarters is in the back."

Santana thought for a second. They had two and a half bedrooms in the apartment. The half was a tiny out-of-the-way room, only large enough for a desk or a chair and TV. It had to be the size of a large walk-in closet or oversized bathroom. "You mean the storage room?" She shook her head, walking away in disbelief. She didn't want an answer or expect one. *This must be what Gully meant by rhetorical.* "Whatever," she mumbled, grabbing her keys from the table and leaving. Her phone chirped before she made it down the apartment building steps. A text from Meka.

YO MANS HAVIN A BBQ @ THE PARK. BE READY IN 5M!

"So your Moms just moved old boy in two weeks ago, and now he has your room?" Pharaoh asked with a chip-tooth smile. He shook his head. "I need to meet him. Sounds like we cut from the same cloth, 'cause he definitely a G."

Santana playfully punched his shoulder, and he leaned back against the car. She looked around at the crowd of people. It seemed like everyone had come out to the picnic, and she knew it was because of Pharaoh's name and reputation of paying for everything. It didn't matter that the whole neighborhood and a few strays showed up, he'd footed the bill and announced all ribs and drinks were on him. "And she bought all the furniture in the office—even the computer. And I've been asking for one—scratch that, I've been *needing* one forever. . . ."

Pharaoh just nodded again. "Don't worry about it. Wit yo mom's reputation, old boy will be out soon. You know that. She won't keep him long."

"I dunno." Santana shrugged. "It seems like he pays how he weighs, and he's a big man."

"So that means he really forking over dat cash."

Pharaoh whistled. "I don't know then, shawty. Homeboy might be there to stay. We'll see. I'll put word out on the skreets, see what he really made of. He a skreet player or a pimp?"

She hunched her shoulders again. "He's not from the streets. I can tell. And he comes home every night. But you know my mom only keeps men with money, so you never know."

"He ain't neither one then. Guess you gone havta ride it out." Pharaoh pulled Santana close, then looked away into the crowd.

"Unless . . . I can always come stay with you."

Commotion broke out behind them, and Pharaoh released her from his embrace. Santana turned her head, following his stare. A group of guys were brawling over what looked like a dice game.

Pharaoh stood up, hocked spit, and cursed. "Man, you can't take these fools nowhere. I swear. I'll be back, shawty. Let me go iron out some of these creases—I godda straighten these fools out."

"Well . . ." she shouted to his back, needing an answer. "You think it's a good idea? Me coming to your house?"

Pharaoh straightened his fitted baseball cap, and slightly shook his head. "We'll talk 'bout it. I gotcha, though. But next week we goin' to the cabins for four days. You comin wit me," he said over his shoulder. It wasn't a question.

Santana leaned against the car and felt the defeat sinking in. She could tell his answer was no even if he hadn't said it. It was cool though, that's what she told herself.

She wasn't one to break. She was much too fly for that. Plus, now she had the getaway to look forward to.

"Meka!" she yelled toward the crowd, spotting her best friend. "Up here."

"Good afternoon, Santana. It's nice seeing you here," Gully's unmistakable voice greeted from behind.

She turned her head and smiled for the first time that day. Gulliver stood behind her with his hands in his checkered golfing-short pockets, and his color-coordinated shirt had a Harvard University emblem embroidered on the chest. He sported leather loafers and no socks. "Hi, Gully. I didn't know you'd be here. Didn't expect you to . . . not with all this mess," she remarked, nodding toward the fight that Pharaoh was breaking up.

"Because of that?" He pointed. "Oh, I'm used to that. I've been around these people my whole life. They're my friends."

Santana leaned against the car, and looked at him in amazement. "Them? *Please.* You way too nice, and— don't take this the wrong way—square, for all this."

Gulliver laughed, long, hard, and genuine. "Don't judge a book. . . . I'm from the same neighborhood, Santana. I was just afforded the opportunity to do things they weren't."

Santana rolled her eyes. "Like what?"

"Private school, summer camps, chess club." He shrugged. "I came from a two-parent household—two parents who worked and were educated before they passed. Then my grandmother raised me, and kept me accustomed to the same lifestyle—well, except for the neighborhood, of course. But that's because she's owned her house since the neighborhood was safe and beautiful." Santana looked at him as if she understood. "Enough of my talk. It's hot out here. Would you like for me to get you a bottled water? Of course you need one. Me too," he said, answering for her and walking toward the lively picnic.

Something heavy hit the back of her head. Instinctively, her hand went to her skull. "Ow." She brought her palm to her face, and bright red blood met her eyes. "What the . . . ?" She turned around and saw Nae and her friends walking her way. Nae had rocks in her hands, and was throwing them at Santana.

"Oh, act bad now!" Nae dared, throwing another one.

Santana didn't answer or hesitate. She dropped her purse, turned up her anger, and ran as fast as she could toward Nae and her flunkies. In seconds, she'd given Nae a speed knot in the middle of her forehead and slammed her on the concrete drive. It never crossed her mind that she could be jumped by the girls who were supposed to be Nae's friends, but had turned out to be spectators—except for one who thought she was a field-goal kicker, and was practicing on Santana's side. Santana held her breath, bracing against the blows the girl was footing into her ribs, and continued to pummel Nae like she was tenderizing a steak.

"Un-un," she heard Meka yell, followed by a heavy thump.

Side by side, Santana and Meka were finishing off their opponents. Santana raised her fist, aiming for Nae's eye, but she missed. A pair of strong hands under her arms lifted her body off the ground and tossed her into some-one's hold.

"Get off me!" Santana spat, kicking her feet, trying to get back to the whipping she was putting on Nae. "That scallywag hit me in the back of the head with a rock."

Meka got up off the girl on the ground, leaving her balled up in fetal position, crying like a baby. "Yeah, and this . . . this—whatever, jumped in."

Pharaoh stood between Santana and Nae. A calm rage covered his face.

"Get," Santana hissed, wiggling. "Off. Me!"

"Okay, Santana," Gulliver said, releasing her. "I was only trying to—"

"Nae!" Pharaoh boomed, quieting the thickening crowd who'd gathered. "What I tell you, shawty?" He reached into his pocket, took out his keys, and tossed them to Gully. He turned back to Nae. "Didn't I tell you," he said through gritted teeth, "that I was gone slap yo daddy?" He turned to Santana. "Gully's gone take you home, shawty, and I'm gonna come scoop you later. Gully fill her in on the rest."

"But Pharaoh . . ." Santana began.

He looked at her and shook his head. "Yo, I need somebody to give me a ride, and somebody else to give Nae a ride and follow behind me. I want her to be there so she can see me slap her daddy."

Santana rode for miles in silence. She had no words, she was much too angry to speak. She didn't know how or why it all happened, and couldn't figure out why Nae and her flunkies felt welcome enough to attend Pharaoh's picnic. Gulliver cruised along at his usual thirty-five miles per hour, acting as if nothing had happened. Santana looked at him from the corner of her eye, and wondered when he became her official chauffer.

"Guess you think I was wrong?" she said, watching as he turned the corner and cruised up her block.

He shook his head. "I'm not here to judge you, Santana. But you are too pretty and smart to be fighting. But if she hit you in the head with a rock . . . the Constitution says we have a right." He pulled in front of her apartment building, and put the car in park. He unfastened his seat belt, then got out of the car and walked to her door and opened it, extending his hand to her. "One sec," he said, pressing the car remote, popping the trunk, and half jogging to it. "Here," he called for her.

Santana met him behind the car with her brows raised.

He handed her a heavy shopping bag. "What's this?"

Gulliver took the bag from her. "I'll take this for you. It's too heavy." He patted the bag. "It's your computer—the gift from Pharaoh."

"Really!" Santana squealed and smiled again for the second time that day.

" 'Ey you!" her mother's voice called from the balcony. " 'Ey you! Cute, nerdy-looking boy. Come up here and do me a favor."

"Sorry. That's my mother—she won't tell you that though. She's going to pretend to be my sister."

The front door opened before they reached the apartment, and her mother stuck her head out. "Santana, close your eyes, honey. Craig and I have a surprise for you."

Honey? Craig and I? When did she start talking like that? Oh my gawd, I can only imagine what it is. Santana looked over her shoulder at Gulliver, and thought it best that she play along. She didn't want him to know how dysfunctional her family life was, not after he'd shared his stable two-parent-household story. She had no idea why she cared what he thought of her, but she did. Playing into her mother's game, she shut her lids and allowed her mother to guide her through the house.

"Surprise!" her mother yelled.

Santana opened her eyes and relief coursed through her. She was back in her old room, and everything was exactly where it had been before except for her girly-pink paint. But she could live with the new sueded shade of chocolate. In fact, it made her feel more grown up.

"I thought you'd like your room back. This is your home—our home, and I'd really like us to be a family," Craig said, then offered his hand to Gulliver. "I'm Craig. What's your name, son? And what do you do . . . ?" His voice trailed off as he zeroed in on the collegiate emblem on Gully's shirt. "You're a Harvard man, too?" He looked at Santana's mother. "I don't know if you're right, sweetheart. I think Santana has pretty good taste in boys—a Harvard man like me, I like that!" He patted Gully on the back. "Yes, sir!"

Twenty-two. Pharaoh's never been here to meet my mother. Santana watched as Gulliver and Craig talked about college and sports, then headed off to move the china cabinet for her mother, and set up her computer and work on a database for Craig. She wished that Pharaoh was more like Gully. Maybe that was why she didn't correct Craig for thinking that she and Gully were together. That's what she told herself.

9

PATIENCE

Patience sat at her desk pretending to study her weekly sunday school lesson and thought about Pretty Boy. It'd been almost two weeks since she'd seen him or Silky, and it was driving her nuts. All she'd been able to do was pass coded telephone messages through Silky, telling him she'd be able to see him soon. And soon had finally come—at five o'clock, the time Bishop had told her her punishment would officially be over. A smile spread on her face because it could've been worse. She'd slipped into her house and room right before her parents had come home that Sunday, so the grounding had been minimal because no one could prove what time she'd come home. Her eyes moved across the room and admired the LV bag sitting atop the dresser. She had no idea how she'd continue to hide it from the Bishop, but she had to come up with something. Her having such an expensive purse was equal to blasphemy in his eyes, though his and her mother's purchases made the Louis's price seem discount-store cheap. Her eyes scanned the room and landed on her roomy walk-in closet. Her shoes were hidden in there, as were her sunglasses. She'd carefully tucked them away. They were in a plastic shopping bag, tied to the hanger inside the fluffy, outdated, lollipop-kid Easter dress she'd been forced to like and model at the annual Easter Celebration, which had been a clever title for a fashion show.

The telephone buzzed, causing her to jump. Before the first ring ended, she'd picked up. She'd been denied too many calls by letting the staff or her family answer, and she wouldn't let that happen again, at least not while her parents were at the church and she was free.

"Hey, BFF . . . can you talk? I need help with the sunday school lesson. I got a lot of catching up to do, and I want to study before we get back on Saturday," Silky lied, talking in code, stretching her fabrication to include being out of town.

Patience breathed a relieved sigh, glad she'd answered before anyone else did. "Yes, I can help. I'm a little busy studying myself, but tell me where you're stuck, and I can call you and walk you through it later. Okay?"

"I'm in the New Testament . . ."

The new house. Check. Patience took a mental note.

". . . John 3:30. 'He must become more, I must become less.' You know the lesson?"

3:30. Can I come then?

Patience smiled. She was glad she and Silky had come up with a code language; otherwise they'd never see each other, though Silky didn't know it. "Yes, I know it." *I can come.* "I'll call you as soon as I can. Have your study materials ready," she threw in just in case there was another ear on the line, which she'd learned to assume there always was.

The taxi seat was sweaty, Patience found out when she got out of the car and her thighs smacked loose from the navy pleather, leaving an oily print. Almost skipping, she made her way up Silky's sidewalk, breathing easier. She'd left the house as quietly as she could, walked through the backyards of her neighbors until she made it to the other side of the block, then quick-footed her way to the neighborhood gas station and called the taxi. She rang the doorbell, then looked at her watch. Early. 3:28.

Her heart forgot to stop beating when he answered the door. Pretty Boy. Trill. That was the stage name everyone knew him by, she assumed. Everyone but her. Sure, she'd heard her worldly on-the-low-low sisters quietly whispering about concerts they'd snuck to and parties they'd attended, but she didn't know who the celebrities they oooed and ahhed over were. She shrugged. She'd probably even heard one of his songs while riding with them in the car before they muted the volume, warning her not to tell the good Bishop. Yes, Trill was his name, that's what he'd finally told her in the mall, but she'd never asked what his parents had put on his birth certificate. She didn't care. All that mattered to her was that she could call him and he'd answer. Still, she wondered what Trill meant, but she wouldn't question him on that either. She was green enough as it was; she didn't want to seem fluorescent green.

"S'up, lil momma? Why you shrugging? You ain't happy to see me?" He flashed that crooked smile that made her knees weak, then stepped to the side to allow her entrance.

Her lips spread into a full grin, and she nervously bit her bottom lip as she walked by him.

"A'ight then! I see I make you feel that way too?" he said, throwing her off course.

"Huh?" she said, while she waited for him to close the door so she could follow him. She was at Silky's, but, for some reason, she felt she needed to wait for him like it was his domain.

Trill stopped in his tracks, bent forward, and planted his lips on her cheek. "I can tell you want me, lil momma. Nibbling on your lip like that. That's a sexy move."

Patience stiffened, pulling her lips inside her mouth. She didn't realize that she'd made a move on him. She hadn't even realized she'd bit her lip. Blushing now, she forgot why she was there. Oh. Silky. "Sorry, I didn't mean—"

" 'Bout time you got here!" Silky exclaimed and saved her, waltzing into the room with the Growler in tow. "Kisses," she said, blowing an air kiss at Patience, then opened the door. "We're leaving. But you good, Trill got you. See you on the red carpet."

Patience crinkled her eyebrows. She'd just got there, and Silky was leaving? "Wait . . ." She spoke too late. The front door closed while her hand was midair trying to hail her friend. "I thought . . ."

Trill wrapped his hand around Patience's waist and pulled her to him. "I got you, P. No need to worry." His cell phone began to vibrate on his hip. He removed it from the clip, scrolled around on the screen, then said, "Our driver's out front."

She was in another stretch before she could question it. Again, they weren't alone. A coal-black and very elegant woman who weighed all of eighty pounds, sat across from them, snapping on someone on the phone. Upon closer inspection, Patience saw that she was a natural beauty who wore no makeup and had super-sized feet.

"Get it together! Now!" She paused, flipped through a stack of files on her lap, selected one, and put it on top of the pile. She looked at Patience and smiled. "What size do you wear, darlin'?"

"Five." Patience watched as the woman wrote her name in capital letters on the file in permanent marker, flipped it open, and began scrawling her clothes size on a sheet of paper in it. *I have my own file? Wow!* She eyed the woman's lap, saw that her file was on top of a bright orange one marked DAMAGE CONTROL!

"Five!" the tiny woman boomed into the cell. Then back to Patience, "Shoe size?"

"Seven . . . ?" Patience's answer rolled out of her mouth sounding more like a question because she'd almost been afraid to speak, but the woman warmed every time she looked her way.

"Seven . . . no, not seven and a half. Seven!" She added Patience's shoe size to the file. "You need to switch cell carriers because your phone and reception are garbage. Gar-bahg!" The lady paused again, scooted to the edge of her seat, and beckoned Patience to move closer. Her tiny hand was on Patience's face in seconds, moving her jaw left and right, then turning her head so she could examine Patience's hair. "A fairly good amount," she said, nodding in appreciation. She turned her attention back to the person she was verbally assassinating on the phone. "We're going to need Janine." Pause. "Nooo! Not Janey. Ja-neen! Got it? Last time you sent Janey. I want Ja-neen!" She powered off her cell, then shot her eyes at Patience. She sighed heavily. "I'm Countess, your new best friend, slash stylist, slash nutritionist, slash media guru!" she said, chipperly.

Patience wondered if Countess was what people considered bipolar. She'd flip-flopped between angry and bubbly within a split second, and Patience had never met anyone like her. "Yes, ma'am," was all she could say. She didn't want to risk upsetting her.

The car turned into a long tree-lined driveway, and coasted for a while before halting to a stop. "A'ight," Trill said, leaning over and kissing her on the cheek. "I'll see you in a minute, lil momma . . . and relax. Countess's got you." He opened the car door himself and got out.

"Where—" she began, watching him walk toward what appeared to be a small house.

"Haircut three times a week," Countess said as the car pulled away. "So . . . who are you? Verbal resume, please."

Patience froze when the car pulled off. "Ma'am?" The trees blurred as they whizzed by them, making it hard for Patience to count them as she was desperately trying to do. She wanted to concentrate on something else besides Countess sitting across from her staring into her soul.

"*Ma'am?*" Countess raised her perfectly arched brows and broke out in hearty laughter. "Ma'am?" she repeated.

"Wow . . . someone with manners. Finally. Thank you, God! He's good!" She threw up her hands.

Patience looked at her out of the corner of her eye, and watched Countess relax and soften. "Yes, He is. All the time!"

Countess's head spun quickly, and a genuine smile brightened her face. "You're different, Patience. You're different, and I think we just might really get along. Tell me something. Is Patience really your name?"

Patience nodded.

"Odd, but I like it. What's your last name?"

"Blackman."

Countess's eyes stretched wide, and her whites appeared brighter than normal because of the darkness of her skin. "Patience Blackman . . ." Her brows shot up in thought. "Patience Blackman . . . as in Bishop Blackman's daughter. *The* Bishop Blackman? I thought you looked familiar. I haven't been to service in over a year, but I kind of remember you."

Reluctantly, Patience nodded again. She knew admitting she was Bishop's daughter could be her downfall, but she was too afraid to lie to Countess for fear of her switching attitudes again.

Countess perked up. "One minute, darlin'." She whipped out her cell phone and called someone. "Cancel Janine! Cancel her! We're going to need Francoise. Yes—Trill's Francoise. This isn't just a date, this is press. This is huge!"

Patience wondered what she was talking about, and hoped she could find a way to ask Countess not to tell her father.

The car stopped and the door opened. Countess grabbed her hand and pulled her from the car. "Let's go!" she rushed her, pulling her up the walk. The house that stood before her was as big as her own, and had five luxury cars and two motorcycles in the circular driveway. Heavy bass rattled the windows, and smoke lingered from the inside when Countess opened the front door. "Up the stairs, quick!"

" 'Ey!" Some guys she'd never seen before greeted them from the right, where a crowd of people filled a huge room.

"Un-uh!" Countess shushed them, snapping and pointing her finger at them like a weapon. "This is her. Her! Trill's her that he warned you to stay away from. I'll tell—and you don't want that." She gently grabbed Patience by her shoulders and veered her toward a grand staircase. "We're running out of time."

Patience climbed the staircase, unsure of what was going on and wondering what they were running out of time for. She gathered her breath and thoughts when they'd made it to the top of the landing and stopped suddenly. Gold and platinum CDs housed in shadow-box frames were everywhere. She imagined this is what the inside of record companies looked like. Posters. Studio shots. Photos from award shows with Trill holding up heavy awards. He was everywhere, and his images showed the same thing. Trill was a superstar.

Hands clapped loudly, pulling her attention.

"Ahh, Patience. So lovely. Cheekbones to die for. Natural beauty and hair—like Countess, she abhors makeup and flat out refuses to wear it. You're also a blank canvas, or you were minutes ago," a very coiffed and elegant man sang, extending his hand. "I'm Francoise—your beauty god. And honey, I'm going to make you into a walking miracle."

Patience took Francoise's hand and smiled. Immediately, she felt at ease with him. She didn't know if it was his compliments, genuine nature, or the power he oozed, but whatever it was about him, she welcomed it. After all, she guessed he had to be more stable than Countess. Patience followed Francoise to an open door, looked over her shoulder at Countess, and watched her transform back into a petite bulldog.

The room was filled with women dressed in all black, looking like a Paul Mitchell commercial. Racks of women's clothes lined one wall; a hair station was on another, complete with a washbowl and dryer. A makeup vanity with a comfortable-looking chair sitting in front of it held more face paint than Patience had ever seen. Oh. God. There was even a mani-pedi station with a whirlpool foot bath in the corner. "Wow."

"Wow is right. This is all for you, Patience. Trill must really like you, honey. I've never seen this happen before. Well, besides for him." He clapped his hands twice. "Off you go. Bathroom's over there. Take a quick shower and put on the cotton robe on the door hook. I'll see you in twenty."

She was nervous, but she went anyway. What other choice did she have? She guessed she could've questioned it, but didn't see the point. How many times would she have like this in her life with a posse of people who were there just to cater to her? No one else. Just her. She disrobed, turned on the shower, and stepped under the spray. *Take this, Bishop. You're wrong; every boy doesn't just want the cow's milk. I believe this one wants the cow.*

10

SANTANA

Santana gripped her real-looking faux Gucci silencer bag next to her side. It'd been a minute since she and Meka had been boosting, and her summer wardrobe was a dead giveaway. She'd worn two shirts from last season, and it was putting a major dent in her swag. Her eyes darted around as they headed to the glass-enclosed bank of elevators in the underground parking lot. Phipps Plaza had too much security and undercover officers to be a quick and easy hit, and she felt it in her soul.

"I don't know about this, Meka. Something don't feel right."

Meka strutted and tossed back her lace-front wig as if she'd grown the hair herself. "Girl, it's good. You just feel like that because we doing higher-quality stores this time. You just godda have a higher-quality attitude. You deserve this, you own this," she encouraged, pushing open the glass door and hopping on an awaiting elevator.

Santana huffed. "Okay. I'm gonna trust you, Meka."

Meka side-eyed her and puckered out her pouted glossy lips. "You always do. And why wouldn't you? I gotcha back! Come on. Gucci first, then Louis."

Santana reluctantly followed Meka. She slowed her usual walk, and took her time. She was in no rush to go to jail, and the smell of barred cells and fingerprints was in the air. Gucci awaited them with a wide door, a moderately filled room, and overfriendly staff. Santana watched as Meka zeroed in on a cute sales guy with a bright smile and warm demeanor. From a distance they looked like friends, but Santana knew better because she knew Meka. And Meka didn't socialize—especially when she was boosting. If anything, they knew to keep attention off them.

"Ooh, can I see that one?" Meka asked, pointing to a bag.

The guy nodded, turned, and grabbed the purse, handing it to her. "That'll be on sale . . ." He stopped, looked around to see if anyone was watching or listening. ". . . . tonight," he whispered.

Santana averted her eyes, then drifted out of the store to answer a call. " 'Ey Baby!" she cooed into the phone, "I'm almost ready. Just here at the mall picking up a few new 'fits for the trip. What time are we leaving?"

"Soon as I finish up some bidness, about seven-somethin'."

Santana looked at her watch. She had almost eight hours to shop and pack. "Cool. I can't wait!"

"Me too, shawty. You got yo man all to yo'self for four whole days. What you gone do wit that?"

Santana smiled. "Wait and see. I'll call you back when I'm ready, baby."

"You on the phone having a make-out session?" Meka quizzed, laughing. "That Pharaoh got you on straight lock. If I was you, I'd pick me up a lil somethin'-somethin' sexy wear. Ya heard?" Meka said, headed toward Louis Vuitton. "You can pick up something in the store connected to it. They have some pretty stuff."

Santana smirked, following behind Meka. Picking up some cute lounge wear was exactly what she would do. She guessed coming to Phipps wasn't a bad idea after all. "I'm gonna go in here and cop some cute pieces."

Meka nodded and headed toward the Louis store. "Meet me in here if you finish first, and vice versa. Ooh," she cooed like she was in love. "My girl's working in here today. I'm gonna clean up!"

Santana walked through the store until she made it to the juniors section. She yawned, bored with the little-girl gear they offered. Didn't they know that teenagers liked luxurious wear like grown-ups? Everybody didn't do pink and frilly.

"Whatever," she said aloud, turning toward the women's section, sure she'd find something there. She felt fabrics, fingered the lace, and found she didn't like their stuff either. Maybe it was just the store, she thought, then headed out to meet Meka in Louis.

Before she could step foot inside the store, she spotted Meka in the back by the luggage. She seemed to be in deep conversation with a female sales associate. *She's racking up,* crossed her mind as she wondered how much

Meka would have to pay the girl for whatever it was she was getting.

"They didn't have nothing. . . ."

Meka whipped her head toward Santana and made a face. Santana drew her eyebrows together. *What's she saying?* Again, Meka screwed her face, then slightly turned her head.

"What?" Santana whispered, watching her best friend. "Oh . . ." Now she got it, Meka didn't want her to mess up her play. Santana turned around to leave and ran smack dead into a huge policeman's chest.

"Her, too!" someone said. "I saw them come in together. She's an accomplice."

"Happy it ain't me." Santana looked around for the person they were talking about, glad it couldn't be her because today she hadn't stolen anything. But a quick grab of her shoulder and the double clink of handcuffs being slapped on her wrists, told her three things: She didn't know what she was talking about, you didn't have to steal to be taken into police custody, and there was nothing fly about crime. She was guilty by association.

Her head hurt, and her butt felt flat as a pancake. She'd been sitting in the hard plastic chair for a short eternity. After being asked her name and parents' information, she'd been held in a room that looked like something she'd seen on a cop show on television. Dull beige concrete walls, two-way mirror, table with three chairs, tape and video recorder, and WANTED Crime Stoppers posters on the back of the closed door. She shook her head, then placed it in her hands. She didn't know how she'd gotten here, not today. She'd gone boosting, sure, but she hadn't stolen anything and wasn't able to find out what Meka had taken. In fact, she hadn't been allowed to see or talk to Meka.

The door opened and a female officer walked in. She grabbed one of the chairs, slid it to her, and straddled it.

"What have you learned, Santana?" The officer's tone was dry.

The watch on the officer's arm read 4:47. *Good.* If they let her go now like she thought they would, that meant she had enough time to make it to Pharaoh.

"Do you hear me?" the officer repeated.

Santana just looked at her. The woman must've been out of her tree, or just didn't know any better. There was no way Santana was going to talk to her. People didn't talk where she came from. That was the code of the streets. *Hear no evil, speak no evil, see no evil.* Santana was sure the "no evils" came from somewhere else— she'd heard about them at school—but they also applied to the hood. If you heard something, you pretended you didn't. If you knew of someone doing wrong, you didn't speak on it. And if you saw something, you turned a blind eye. So Santana decided she'd be deaf, mute, and blind.

"All right," the officer gave in, rising off the chair. "You'll be back, trust me. I see girls like you come in here all the time. You get to go today, but we have a revolving door." She waved her hand, beckoning Santana. "Come on, your family has come to get you."

Santana got up and sucked her teeth as loud as she

could. How dare the officer assume she'd be back? *That's what's wrong with the system,* she thought. Authority always condemned, then wondered why you couldn't be saved.

"I betcha a dollar to a dime, you won't see me again. Did it ever cross your mind that I didn't do anything wrong—that's why I was held and not charged?"

The officer waved her away. "You did something wrong, even if it was just picking the wrong friend to hang out with. Go pick up a book."

To Santana's surprise, Gully was waiting for her. He had his face in his hands, but she could spot him anywhere. The same leather loafers minus socks, shorts above the knees, and a crisp polo shirt were three giveaways.

"Gully?" Santana called out to him. "What're you doing here? I thought I had to have an adult sign me out."

Gulliver stood, straightening the creases in his shorts. Worry was etched in his face. "An adult did—your mother. She had something to do so she asked me to wait for you and take you home."

Something to do? Santana was angry and relieved. Upset because everything was more important to her mother than Santana, and she was relieved because she didn't want her mother to slap her teeth on the jailhouse floor for embarrassing her.

"Okay, and before you ask, I don't want to talk about it. I didn't steal nothing or break any laws."

*   *   *

As Santana unlocked her front door, she wondered why Gully was behind her. Just as she requested, he hadn't said a thing to her on the entire ride home. But he did keep looking at her as if he wanted to, and his stare had made her uncomfortable because she felt see-through.

"Come in," Craig said, sitting on the middle seat on the sofa. "Gulliver, please wait on us in my office. This will only take a minute."

Santana's eyes rolled in her head. First her mother had appointed Gully as her ride; now she'd somehow given Craig stepdaddy rights. She could just feel a father-daughter talk brewing. But there was a problem. She didn't have a father, and unless Craig had gone half on a baby girl with some other woman, he certainly didn't have a daughter.

Sure enough, he patted the seat next to him. "Let's talk, Santana. Come have a seat."

Because he'd been respectful to both her and her mother, had given her room back, and had gone out of his way to make the trio feel like a family, Santana sat. Just not next to him. She tossed her purse on the floor, and plopped down in the chair.

"What's up?" she asked, then stared at a spot over his head to avoid his eyes.

He paused and exhaled. "I volunteered to talk to you for your mother. Look at me, Santana. . . . As I said, I volunteered because your mother's upset and we're both highly disappointed." He threw up his hands, and laughed a little. "But you know what, Santana? This isn't your fault, not entirely."

Her eyes zoomed in on him. Finally, someone understood.

"It's your environment. Where you live, go to school, who you hang out with." He nodded in agreement with himself. "But all that's going to change. Today while you were in Phipps or jail, I was in my attorney's office closing on a house for us. A house in a wonderful, safe neighborhood, in one of the best school districts—but that doesn't count because you'll be going to a very elite, year-round preparatory school to ready you for college."

"Huh?" Her jaw went south again, but not because someone had taken her bedroom furniture and moved it. It hung because they were trying to take away her life. "Huh?"

Craig nodded and smiled. He was clearly pleased with himself. "Yes, you heard right. We're a family now, and as a man it's my job to take care of my family."

Santana just stared at him.

"And that's why your mother and I've decided that you're on punishment. So wherever you've packed your bag to go, you can consider cancelled. Oh, and that computer that was in your room—it's gone. My guy Gulliver is going to help you build your own computer. That's how you can redeem yourself and prepare for your new school." He held out his hand. "And your mother wants your phone."

11

DYNASTY

"Rufus, I'm telling you, those girls were squabbling!" Dynasty's voice rose as she punched her fist in her palm. "Straight getting it in. It was like one minute, yo"—she put her fist in her hand again—"then the next . . . *word.*"

She sat on the bench of the raggedy picnic table telling him about the fight she'd seen when she and City went to the barbecue while Sheeka, an almost mute neighborhood kitchen beautician who could hear, but couldn't speak, braided her hair. She shook her head despite Sheeka trying to make her be still. It was just hard to believe the nice girls who'd sold City the clothes he'd bought her could be so brutal. As soon and she and City pulled into the park looking for a parking space, out of nowhere the girl named Santana blew by them and punched some girl in the face.

"I swear, Rufus, the way Santana was beating up that girl you'd swear she had batteries taped to her palms. Then her home girl jumped in when the other girls tried to jump Santana. After that"—she waved her hand in front of her neck in a cutting motion—"dead. Santana and Meka deaded that. Then some dude named Pharaoh—Santana's boyfriend—went to beat up somebody's daddy. He was cute too—Pharaoh, not the daddy."

Rufus made a face. "You stupid."

Dynasty looked at Rufus, and would've kicked herself if she could. Every time she tried to be nice to him, show him some attention so he wouldn't have to fake a heart problem to get noticed, he pulled a turncoat move on her.

"You know what, Rufus? You got two faces, and ain't neither one of them cute. You're just jealous." She turned away from him and picked up her dictionary while Sheeka made a sound indicating she was laughing and popped her in the head with the comb as a way of telling Dynasty to stay still. Dynasty flipped the pages and scanned through the As. "Asinine: stupid." She slid her fingers, swiping the paper until she reached F. "Foolhardy: stupid."

"I know you ain't talking about me, Dynasty. You're the stupid one. You're so stupid you forgot how to be yourself. Ever since you started hanging with City, you talk like him. When did you get excited about a fight? And start saying 'yo' and 'word' and 'deaded'?"

She shut the dictionary, then deadpanned him when Sheeka finished her last braid. Without taking her eyes off Rufus, she paid Sheeka, and gave her a big hug as a way of saying thanks. "I'll see you in a couple of weeks to get the front tightened up, okay?"

Sheeka nodded, pocketed the money, and began collecting the leftover fake hair and braiding supplies.

Dynasty flung her braids over her shoulder. "So, I sound like City now? Well, better than sounding like you, Dufus. So since I sound like City, let me use one of his words when I say this. Here's your *gem*—that's City's word for a gift of wisdom—gem, pearl, jewel. You get it. Your gem: Asinine—stupid. Foolhardy—stupid, and Rufus is—guess what?—stupid, too."

Sheeka made her laughing sound as she made her way down the walk. She stomped her foot to get both Dynasty's and Rufus's attention, then waved.

Rufus put his hand on his hip, then pretended to toss hair over his shoulder. He was mocking her. "Well at least I'm in good company, 'cause you're stupid, too. 'Least I'm not the one acting like I got this and that 'cause I got some new books and clothes—that I'm gonna have to pay for . . . without cash, but something that rhymes with it!"

Dynasty's head almost fell off from Rufus hitting her with his nonsense again. "I don't have to sleep with anybody, Rufus! Are you serious? Is that all you think about?" She shrugged. "I guess you'd have to 'cause don't nobody—especially me—want you."

"I'm telling you this 'cause we're *friends*. People don't do stuff for you for nothing. What you expect from him? He's Pork Chop's grandson, so you know he probably gonna be greasy and sleazy just like Pork Chop. That's why Pork Chop's name is *Pork Chop*. He a big old greasy, sleazy pig."

"And that means what? My momma's name is Lipstick 'cause she outlines her lips *way* outside of her natural lip line and wears more lipstick than Maybelline wears makeup. But do you see me doing the same thing—wearing a ton of paint on my mouth?"

"If I'm stupid, you're naive. Betcha you didn't think I knew that word. But you watch! He's gonna hurt you or run game on you. City is slick just like the city," he said, getting off the table and shuffling toward the sidewalk. "And you better not tell him I said so. . . ."

"Why, you scared?" yelled Dynasty, looking at her dollar-store watch. City told her he'd be by at four o'clock, and she needed to get dressed. There was no way she was going to make him wait, especially after he invited her to an overnight getaway party being held at a cabin. She didn't know how she was going to pull it off, but she had to. He'd also alluded to having a job for her. A real one.

Rufus raised a power-to-the-people fist into the air, then flipped up his middle finger. "Bet you'll need me first . . . and *stupid* me won't be there. Watch yourself, your Aunt Makeup—oops, I mean Maybelline—is on her way, and she has a beer in each hand and mismatched shoes on. Maybe City can buy you a medicine dispenser to keep her brain tight."

Dang. She saw her aunt waiting by the corner of the building, peeking around like she was spying on someone. She jumped back, then looked again. Then did it a third time. Dynasty knew Rufus was right. Her aunt

couldn't have taken her medicine, and Dynasty was starting to suspect her aunt was more than bipolar.

"Dynasty! Get over here and bring my shoes," Aunt
Maybelline yelled, walking into sight.

Dynasty looked down at her feet like she'd forgotten
what shoes she had on, and sure enough, her tennis shoes
were still there. "Ma'am?" she called, walking toward
her aunt, and figuring out a way to go with City. "Do
you need me to help you find your shoes before I go to
school?" She figured she might as well have fun.

Aunt Maybelline waited for her, then worked her heft
to their apartment steps. She looked back at Dynasty,
and she saw that her aunt's eyebrows were drawn on
crooked. One was in a high arch, the other was a straight
line. She put an unlit cigarette to her lips and inhaled,
held in the nonexistent smoke, then blew.

"School? It's summer." She stepped into the apartment.

Dynasty followed her aunt inside. "You know I'm
going to sleepaway camp for the weekend with the Winchester Hills Prep School—the one I've been trying to get
into. You signed the permission slip *last* week. And if I
don't go"—she shrugged—"there may not be any prize
money or lifetime supply of beer. You know the Beer for
Life contest?"

Aunt Maybelline held her face down, then looked sideways at Dynasty under the high-arched brow. Her super-
long fake lashes fluttered.

"Prize money . . . prize money . . . a Beer for Life . . ."
She smiled, then pulled on the unlit cigarette again.
"That's right. I almost forgot. A Beer for Life just like the

lottery, Win for Life! Well, you better hurry up then."
Then her aunt froze as if something had registered.
"Wait, how are you gonna get beer if you're only thir-
teen. Didn't you just turn thirteen?"

Dynasty's breath caught in her throat, but then she remembered who she was talking to. Opening her mouth
wide, she forced herself to laugh. She reached over and
kissed Aunt Maybelline on the cheek, hoping none of the
cream rouge rubbed off on her lips. "Ma'am you are too
funny! I'll take that as a compliment, though. You know
I'm eighteen, I just look thirteen. But, we got good genes.
Huh? Don't worry about it. Remember the permission
slip said you'd win and have to sign for the beer at Mr.
Curtis's store. No one's giving me alcohol!" She jogged
up the stairs and made her way through the maze of stuff
on the floor, so she could pack her bag. City wouldn't
have to wait.

The drive had taken a while, but finally they'd made it.
Stepping out of the car, Dynasty looked around just as
she did on the way. She couldn't believe people lived like
this. Everything was so quiet and peaceful. There were
no corner boys, drugs addicts, or homeless people with
signs. She'd never ventured out this far. The farthest she'd
been was to Alpharetta, and that was only because of
City.

"You ready, Dynasty?" he asked, taking a duffel bag
from the backseat. "We got work to do, people to meet,
places to go. Time for us to get this money, honey." He
licked his lips, and made her wonder if they tasted like
chocolate, the way his skin looked. "You can leave your

bag in the car—we got everything we need right here."
He patted the bag. "Oops, can't forget my magic." He
popped the trunk, went into it, then closed it. He held up
a bottle with gold foil on top.

Champagne?

The door opened before they could knock. Pharaoh,
Santana's boyfriend, gave City a pound, then ushered
them inside. It took all Dynasty had in her not to ask him
where his girlfriend was. She wanted to see her, show off
the hundred-dollar jeans and strapless shirt Santana had
picked out. They'd bought the outfit from her, so she felt
styled by her. In the corner, she spotted Meka, and was
glad that she had someone other than City to talk to.
There seemed to be dozens of guys in the house, and she
knew City would wind up hanging with them, though
she hoped not. But if that did happen, at least there was
one familiar face besides Pharaoh's in the house.

City kept the duffel bag close to his side, patting it
every now and then as he spoke to Pharaoh. Dynasty
stood by his side, not knowing what else to do. She nodded hello over and over again as people made their way
over to them. She could tell Pharaoh was the host of the
party, but City was the celebrity.

"So what y'all drinking on?" Pharaoh asked as some
girl slid under his arm.

Dynasty's eyes bulged, then shot toward where Meka
was standing. Meka gave her a knowing look and a
crooked smile. She could tell neither could believe what
they were seeing. The girl was the one Santana had
beaten up at the park.

City held up his bottle, popped the cork, then took it

to head, guzzling it down. He handed it to Dynasty, nodding for her to do the same. Was he crazy? she wondered. She didn't drink alcohol.

"Oh, I forgot. . . ." Pharaoh said. "You always come prepared with your drink of choice," he teased in TV commercial voice.

City winked at her. "That's not alcohol, Dynasty. It's imported sparkling cider. Real hustlers don't drink or do drugs." He shot a playful look at Pharaoh. "I'll be right back. Dynasty, walk with me."

She walked next to him, and snuck a whiff of the bottle. Sure enough, he hadn't lied. "What's up?"

He pointed out a few guys. "See them? I got something for them. That's the real reason we're here. We're in and out—we're not spending the night. We don't get down like that. We here to make this paper. Broaden our connections so we can build the dynasty I told you about." He unzipped the duffel, then retrieved a paper bag. "Nod at them, and when they nod back, give them the peace sign. If they nod again, then they're in. We got two for twenty, a set for thirty, and one for five hundred jumping off in here. And now you, miss. You wanted to know how you'd have to pay me back. Well, this is it. You are now into distribution." He patted the top of her head. "I'll be over there talking to my people. You remember Meka?"

Her jaw fell toward the floor. Her stomach turned. She felt like she needed to pee. She couldn't believe Rufus was right. City had only brought her to the party to engage in something illegal. But what could she do? She was with him in the woods, in the middle of nowhere.

12

PATIENCE

Cameras were everywhere. Everywhere. Patience stood next to Trill, unsure of what to do next. She didn't know whether to walk to the left or the right, to look up or away. She'd never before seen an awards show other than a religious one, let alone attend a nationally televised one, complete with red carpet, paparazzi, and a superstar for a date.

"You're a stunner, lil momma." He bent over, wisped her curls from her face and breathed into her ear, "I'm mean you looking so fresh and so clean. Smelling even fresher. You just fresh to death in that yellow, huh? Looking sweet like flowers."

"Trill! Trill! How does it feel to be nominated for so many awards? Do you think you're going to win them all? We're rooting for you." A reporter thrust a mic in their faces.

"Yes," a woman reporter said. "And who's your date, Trill? I don't think we've ever seen you as a duo."

"What's your name, young lady? How does it feel to be around so much black star power?" another yelled.

Patience looked down at her flowing buttercup gown, then fidgeted with the yellow flower in her hair. She carefully moved her feet, hoping her toes wouldn't slide out the front of the gold open-toe strappy stilettos that she was afraid to walk in. She smiled, then set her gaze on Trill for guidance.

He looked at her and flashed that crooked smile. He licked his lips, and politely answered questions as fast at they were thrown at him; then he rocked her world, stunning her. "This"—he wrapped his arm around Patience and squeezed her a little—"beautiful young lady . . . she's my date—but I'm making her my girl. So get used to seeing her, fellas. She's a keeper. Ya heard!" He winked at them, then her, then laced his fingers through hers and led her into the theater. Inside they were escorted to the second row, where his name was taped to his seat.

In minutes, the place had filled with more celebrities than she'd ever seen. She knew they were famous by their names, the attention they drew, and their entourages. One person in particular caught her eye because her father wore his sweat suits and cologne, and had called him a mogul. The lights went down, and someone came to escort Trill to the back of the stage.

"In a minute, lil momma. I'll be back. Your man's godda perform." He sent her an air kiss and left.

Patience watched him disappear, and giddiness claimed

her. She was so happy and excited it was hard for her to sit still. Trill was wonderful and handsome and nothing like what she'd been taught to believe about the opposite sex. More than that, unlike the Bishop, he was available and was truly interested in her.

Just as she was settling, and had killed the want to turn around and stare at all the other stars in the room, someone thumped into Trill's seat. Patience looked to her right, and almost didn't see her because her coal-black skin nearly disappeared in the dark, but there she was. The mood switcher. Countess.

"Ooh," she squealed. "This is so exciting. The Bishop's daughter and Trill. The magazines and radio are going to eat it up! I hope you're ready," Countess cooed, flipping a legal pad on her lap. "Okay. I'm going to need all your stats. Age. Date of birth. Top faves. Peeves. Favorite designer. Last boyfriend—please don't let him be famous."

Patience inhaled, wondering why the lady was all in her business. It didn't take a street or worldly education for her to know Countess was a piece of work, and would have to be taken in doses. She decided to answer the last question first.

"I've never had a boyfriend."

"What? What do you mean by *never*?"

She looked at Countess in the dimness of the theater and repeated herself.

"So you're the *V* word?" she asked, almost salivating. "Fantastic. I can come up with a heck of an angle for that. 'She's saving herself for marriage. Trill's new thrill is real—one-hundred-percent innocent. She's been saving herself for true love.' Isn't that great? True and Real, just like Trill—you know that's what his name means?"

Patience nodded. No, she didn't know, but she did now.

"Countess, call me Patience—not the Bishop's daughter. It's kind of weird and makes me uncomfortable."

Countess clicked her pen, scribbled on the legal pad, and said, "Got it! Next question."

Music filled the room, cutting their soon-to-be-one-sided conversation short. Patience had no plans on answering everything Countess asked. She didn't care who she was, Trill hadn't asked her to do it. Besides, Patience thought, Countess's nosiness was unheard of and downright rude.

"Okay. Got to go. Here. You're going to need this. He's been going crazy not being able to talk to you." She handed Patience a cell phone. Not just any cell phone, but the new one people had waited in line just to buy. It had to be worth at least four hundred dollars.

"You've seen him on TV," an announcer began. "In Hollywood on the big screen. He's earned more awards than any of us can count. This brother here showed us that even though they call his brother a king, he's also cut from royal cloth. Ladies and gentlemen, we're proud to present—the one, the only, true and real Southern gentleman, Trillllll!"

And he appeared, lifted on a device in a cloud of smoke. From where she sat, he looked heavenly. He was dressed in all white from his slightly baggy jeans, to his T-shirt, to his fresh-out-of-the-box Ones he'd bought while they were in the mall. His jewelry was platinum, except for his bejeweled rosary beads with a huge diamond cross. She knew if her father could see him, he'd freak, and say he was exploiting and mocking what was supposed to be a humble religion. *Bishop's not humble either,* she thought, justifying Trill's indulgence. His hands thrust in the air and spread until he looked like a cross himself, and Patience was in awe. She'd never have believed anyone could have more stage presence than her father, but Trill did. Trill was nothing short of electrifying.

"Wow," she whispered, in awe of her date. She couldn't understand what he wanted with her. She was just an innocent little church girl who did her best with the skirts her father demanded she wear. Before tonight, she'd never worn makeup, not even for fashion shows, and her hair was bland. She'd wanted it cut in a style, but her parents didn't believe a woman should cut her locks. So she'd always resorted to a plain ponytail.

"Yeah, dats-what-um-talum'bout." Trill ended one verse and began a next, rapping with country slang and a smooth voice. Patience's eyes stretched in disbelief at his content. He'd always been so polite with her, never saying a tenth of the things he rapped about now. She wondered if he'd done any of the things he was talking about now. Did he have all the ladies? Did he tote guns? He did have a big house, if the house she was at earlier belonged to him, but did he really have many mansions? She tilted her head to the side and wondered what was a doughboy, a trap house, teardrops tatted by someone's eyes? She shrugged, not caring and assuming all his words were just a part of his act. Trill was a good guy and no one could convince her otherwise, not even him or the words that he'd rhymed.

In minutes he was done and sitting back next to her. He smelled like fresh soap, like he hadn't just performed, and was still wearing his whites. "I did okay?"

Patience smiled and nodded. "You were good. Really, really good. I can't believe I've never seen you perform before, but I have heard people singing your song."

He sat back, kicked out his long legs, and put his arm around her. He leaned in, then whispered in her ear. "I'm gonna have you, Patience. I ain't never wanted for much. My brother"—he nodded toward the stage where another rapper was performing—"made sure of that."

Now Patience was really in awe. She knew who the guy on stage was—everybody did. "That's your brother?"

Trill nodded. "I thought you didn't listen to music or watch TV. . . ."

She shook her head no. "But I can see. He's been on billboards throughout the city, the newspaper had an article about his teen outreach, and one Sunday while we were watching Gospel Hour, he was on a wrap-it-up commercial. My sister's one of his biggest fans. She was sad when he went on vacation."

Trill laughed. "Yeah a'ight. *Vacation*—guess that's another term to call the one-year bid he did. He's back though. Back and bigger than ever. You'll meet him later tonight at the private after-party."

After-party? Patience didn't know how she was going to pull off going to an after-party, but she'd find a way. She thought of the phone Countess had given her, and knew that was going to be her way out. She had a few calls to make. First, she'd phone Silky, and then her sister, Hope. If she couldn't reach them, she'd find her cousin Meka. Meka Blackman, the proverbial black sheep of the Blackmans, didn't pull rabbits out of hats—she gamed them out and made them think it was their idea. She was a hustler in every sense of the over used word.

More music blared, bottles of bubbly were popping, and half-naked women danced on stages and poles, some suspended from the ceiling. Mammoth glass sculptures, carefully placed throughout Club Opera, served as dividers, separating relaxing celebrities from the ones who were dancing on the floor. Patience smiled. She was in a club. A real grown-up place with the boy of her dreams. They sat in a section reserved just for Trill and his brother, who was known to the world by the initials T.O.P., or T. Without trying to look at him too hard, Patience saw the resemblance. Caramel skin, clean haircut, and a baby face.

"So, lil momma, my boy here tells me you a good girl. That right?"

Patience nodded, then shrugged. "I guess."

Trill put his arm around her. "No need to be shy, lil momma. You amongst family."

"So . . ." T began, pouring himself and his equally well-known fiancée, Teeny, a drink. "You rap, sing, design? What do you do?"

Patience looked at Trill, blushing. "I just . . . well, study, I guess. But I used to sing in church."

Eyebrows shot up.

"Really? You didn't tell me that you sing," Trill said, sounding something other than just surprised.

Teeny flung her long hair. She scooted closer. "They don't like their women to work—"

"Don't say that," T said to her. "We just like to take care of ours 'cause we're men, and that's what men do. We just don't like our women in the spotlight. It's a grimy business."

Patience laughed. "I don't want the spotlight. Not at all. That's why I stopped singing in the choir. It made me nervous to lead a song and have all those people watching me."

Trill perked up, smiling. Relief crossed his face. He looked at his brother, and they both nodded. "I'm happy to hear that, Patience. Really happy."

"But," Teeny interjected, "she can sing. Has to be able to blow something serious if she was leading songs. I've been to their church, and they have one heck of a choir. Maybe we can use her in the studio. I write songs, Patience. And if you can write the way I think you can sing, we can be the background dynamic duo. Family's important to us, so we work together as a family."

Patience sat there taking it all in. If only her real family could see her now. *Oh God.* She remembered she had to call her sister, and the panic must have registered in her eyes because Trill elbowed her.

"You a'ight?"

She hung her head. "I need to call my sister, see if she'll cover for me. And maybe my cousin Meka, because she'll make my sister do it."

Trill laughed. "Oh . . . I like that. That's kinda raw. Your cousin be strong-arming people. Bet. But it's not necessary. Your sister will cover for you. Believe me. Watch this." He tapped his brother. " 'Ey, T, I need you to do me a favor, bruh. Can you call Patience's sister and tell her to cover for her, then her cousin—the muscle of the family. Patience's parents are real strict, and I don't want her to get in trouble. I want her to stay here with me."

T nodded, setting his drink down. "I gotcha, shawty. What you need me to say?"

"My sister's your biggest fan, and I'm my cousin's favorite."

"Say no more. Pass me the phone."

Patience relaxed next to Trill and leaned her head on his shoulder. He bent down and kissed her forehead, telling her how pretty she was. She couldn't believe her luck, sitting there next to the guy of her dreams and across from his big brother who'd just sealed a deal with her sister to cover for Patience whenever she needed her to, all for the price of an autographed picture and some backstage passes. He'd solidified it all with Meka for the same price, plus a pair of Louboutin shoes.

"The night is ours, lil momma. You know that?"

Patience nodded. She did now.

13

SANTANA

Her life was awful. Santana sat on the edge of her new bed, looking around her new room that was on the second floor of her new home, which was supposed to be a big deal because, as Gully would say, it "bespoke" her new life. She rolled her eyes and her breath caught in the back of her throat. Her life had turned into a Dr. Seuss book. *New this. New that. Newly invented mother. New Dad.* She could throw up in her own mouth, she was so disgusted.

"I hate it here!" she yelled, kicking her heels against the canopy frame, then grunting in pain. "What teenager has a canopy bed with all the frills and lace? What, do I look ten now that *she* wants to be a mom?" Craig had delivered his promises, punishment and all. But worse, he'd enrolled her in the exclusive Winchester Hills Prep, an all-girl, year-round school.

The phone rang and, instinctively, Santana jumped for it. Then she remembered her cell had been confiscated.

"Honey, you can come down for dinner," her mother's newly pinched voice and newly acquired vocabulary that she'd adopted after the move blared through the intercom. Santana assumed her mom had probably purchased her newness along with the pleated draperies that lined the floor-to-ceiling windows and the "smart" Volvo SUV she had parked in the four-car garage.

"All right, Weezie!" Santana yelled, purposely not pressing the TALK button on the intercom so her mother wouldn't hear her. Since the move, she'd nicknamed her mother and Craig, George and Weezie because she felt as if they'd moved on up, but in reality, only her mom had. She'd finally struck gold, and Craig was her jackpot.

"I godda get out of here." She pushed herself up, then off the high bed, and thumped down on the chilly floor. Again, she rolled her eyes. Central air was another newness she couldn't stand. Who'd want floors that feel like ice? *Craig.*

The carpeted hallway felt good to her feet as she made her way toward the massive staircase, then shuffled down the steps. Her nostrils flared, sniffing the air, trying to figure out what her mom had cooked. All she could detect was tomato sauce, so she knew they'd ordered out for pizza.

"Good evening, Santana," Craig greeted her, walking into the house, setting his keys on a table in the foyer, which he'd stressed was pronounced foy-ay, and putting his briefcase down.

Another new this. "S'up, Craig?" She smiled, antici-pating his finding out whom her mother really was. Her mom wasn't a cook. It wasn't that she couldn't; she just didn't. Pizza. Chinese. Soul food from the Rib Shack. Ro-tisserie chickens from Publix—those "bespoke" her mother's culinary highlights, and Santana knew sooner than later, Craig would learn that his Weezie would need a Florence the housekeeper and cook to be everything he needed in a girlfriend.

Craig smiled back at her. "I'm glad to see you're finally in a good mood. I was worried that you wouldn't come around," he said, then did something that made her cringe. He put his arm around her, pulled her to his side, then kissed her on top of her head. "I understand, though. I was young once."

Santana froze. It wasn't that he'd violated her by being overly friendly like the predators that made the evening news. The problem was . . . there was no problem. He'd treated her like she was his own child, and she'd never had a physical father in her life. *Ill.* Now she knew she'd throw up in her mouth.

Her mother zipped out into the adjoining hall, waving a dish towel in one hand, beckoning Craig to come closer. As soon as he was in her mother's reach, her mom stood on tiptoe and embraced—not hugged—him. Her thin arms barely stretched around his football-player build, while she pecked him on the lips, then kissed him on both cheeks. *Sick.* Santana's eyes bulged. The whole scene looked like a made-for-TV-movie with an extra twist she hadn't expected. On her mother's other hand was an oven mitt. Now she knew someone had dropped her off in Lala Land of the Make Believes.

"Come. Come," her mother waved after releasing Craig. "I made some ziti, and I can't wait for you guys to taste it. It's simply delish."

You guys? Delish? This has to be someone else who just looks like my mother, Santana thought. *Definitely Weezie.*

"Oh no, honey. It's just me and you tonight," Craig announced, shocking both Santana and the woman who was parading around in her mother's body. Both of their eyebrows shot to the ceiling, and Craig smiled. "Santana's going to do some work for me with Gulliver. He's outside waiting."

"Work?" both sang in unison.

"Sure. She's going to help him build the databases, and we'll all benefit from it—especially Santana. It'll give her a head start on her computer classes at the school . . . and"—he shrugged—"if all goes well, I may just put her on payroll." He winked at Santana, then turned to her mother. "She's a smart girl, honey. We just have to trust her."

Santana hiked up her low-rise jeans over her butt, then smiled. Yes, they'd just have to trust her, all right. Trust that as soon as she hit the front door she was headed for her old hood so she could find Pharaoh and see when Meka was due to be released from juvy. She felt bad then. Here she was hating all the newness and luxury she'd been surrounded in for a couple of weeks, and her best friend was sitting in a cold juvenile detention cell somewhere for shoplifting. If Meka were there, Santana knew she'd tell her to ride her wave of luck until the tires fell off.

"So?" Santana sang to her mom, pouting her lips and lowering her eyes. She tried to woo her mother with a baby face, hoping it'd make her agree with Craig.

Her mother put her hand on her right hip, poked out her lips too, then looked from Craig to Santana, then back to him again. "All right . . . I guess. But you better help Gulliver *and* listen to him. He's a good young man who's going to go very far. He's the one you need to fol-low behind, not—"

The front door closed behind Santana before her mother could finish. It was as if she'd grown wheels on the bottoms of her feet, she'd skated out of there so fast. The freshly cut grass crunched under the weight of her soles as she made her way to Gulliver, who was standing next to his car.

"Oh!" She snapped her fingers, then made a U-turn. She'd been in such a rush, she'd forgotten she was bare-foot.

"I thought you'd need these," Craig said, meeting her in the doorway with a pair of Js.

Santana snatched the sneakers from him with a quick "thanks," then zoomed back to Gulliver's car. She jumped inside, slammed the door shut, then rushed him. "Hurry up before they realize what they've done!"

"Afternoon, Santana. You look great today. Well . . . every day. So where to?"

Santana stared at him as if he had an eye in the middle of his forehead.

"Home."

The vibration of bass met her as soon as they parked on the block. A song by the hottest two Atlanta rappers, Trill and his brother T, banged, making everyone bob their heads to their funky, infectious lyrics. Santana looked to her left. Even Gully was nodding to the music. She hopped out of the car, looking up and down the street. She was looking for Pharaoh's Charger, but didn't see it anywhere.

"Gully, hand me your cell. I need to call Pharaoh, and I haven't gotten my phone back yet—it's still on punishment, I guess."

Gully grabbed his cell from its holster on his khaki Bermuda shorts, eased out of the driver's side like an old man, and handed it to her. Santana laughed. Gully did everything slow. "Here. You can speed-dial him if you like. He's listed under *H*."

"*H*? Why *H*, when his name begins with *P*?"

"Um. Um. Hustler?" His admittance came out more like a question than a statement. He shrugged. "Well, it's true. That's what he is, and that's what he wants to be known as."

"Are you hating on my man, Gully? Or just looking down on him? He ain't no . . . well, he can be more than that. He's Pharaoh, he can do anything."

Gully nodded, then shook his head no. "No. He said he's not going to do or be anything else. And he put his number in my contacts under *H*—for hustler—not me."

Her heart sank a little. She knew Gully was right and wasn't lying. Hustling was Pharaoh's way, his bragging point that he loved to talk about and show off. It was one of the things that made her fall for him. Scrolling through Gully's contacts, she called Pharaoh but didn't get an answer. She dialed again.

"'Ey, Gully, what's poppin?" Pharaoh's smoky voice was music to her ears.

"'Ey baby, it's me."

"Me who? Who dis?" His tone and words were distant, lost like he really didn't know who she was. Had he forgotten her already? It'd only been weeks—well, one week because she'd snuck and called him from home just the other day.

"What do you mean who? How many people call you 'baby,' Pharaoh? It's Santana. Don't make me flip out here on this block."

Pharaoh laughed from the other end. "I know who dis is. I was just playing. Where ya at, and why you on Gully's phone?"

A voice met Santana's ears from Pharaoh's end, and she pressed Gully's cell to her ear as hard as she could trying to make out who it belonged to, but someone, probably Pharaoh, was obviously covering it. She could tell by the muffle and the shuffling sound.

"Who's that, Pharaoh? I know I hear someone else."

"Hold tight. I'll be there to scoop you in ten minutes. Ten. And I told you don't be asking me 'bout my bidness—some stuff you don't need to know. Ya heard?" He clicked off, but not before Santana realized the other voice belonged to a girl.

Santana wiggled in her seat and averted her eyes from Gully's stare. They'd waited ten minutes for Pharaoh just as he'd asked, but he hadn't shown. In fact, she huffed, he hadn't made an appearance, answered when she'd called him over and over again, or returned a call. Somehow the six-hundred seconds she'd been asked to wait had turned into almost two hours. A car zoomed down the block, and Santana almost broke her neck trying to see if it was Pharaoh's, but it wasn't. Just like all the others she'd hoped were his.

"Are you okay, Santana?" Gully asked, still sitting in the driver's seat. She couldn't believe for the life of her why he'd waited with her outside when his grandmother's house was steps away.

"Yes," she lied. "But let's just go. I don't wait on dudes. I'm much too fly for that. He must've forgotten who I am. Let's roll, Gully. Take me somewhere. Anywhere but home."

The campus was a huge stretch of sidewalks and buildings. A sea of college guys dressed in purple and gold and carrying Q paraphernalia demanded her attention. Then she saw the guys in red who held and twirled canes. There were also some men in blue, but she couldn't see them too well because they were too far away.

Wow. She turned to her right, saw girls who were a bit older than her, and wondered who they were. Some had on red. Others wore pink and green, and made a unison call, letting people know who they were. Sisters in blue smiled at her, causing her to smile back—something she rarely did. Exchanging friendly gestures just wasn't something you did with strangers where she was from, especially people who got their Bobbsey twin on and dressed alike. That was frowned upon in the hood.

"You've been here before, right?" Gulliver asked, walking next to her like an old friend. "I thought you'd like to see the step show. It may help lift your spirits after . . ."

Santana nodded, but she hadn't been on a college campus before. She didn't know why she had such a hard time being honest with Gully about simple things like her once-dysfunctional family. She shrugged her shoulders. She could fool everyone else, but not herself. The truth was, she knew Gully was smart and college bound, and that made her feel a little less-than, something she wasn't used to. She was Santana Jackson, the flyest girl in her old neighborhood, so she couldn't feel inferior. She just couldn't.

"This is great," she admitted, when they walked up on the crowd, and watched the show begin. There was a feeling of welcome, excellence, and greatness in the air, and Santana knew it was contagious because it made her wonder for the first time what college would be like.

Then reality began to crash around her. She wasn't built for this—she was barely a C student, and hated school. She'd always been too fly and too good to just sit in a classroom and pay attention—not when she could hang with Pharaoh, boost with Meka, and dress better than her wannabes. She watched the rest of the step show in silence, and felt her ego deflate a little more with each stepper. They were smarter than her, some prettier, and most of the guys didn't look twice at her. Santana looked down at her half shirt, too tight and too little, low-rise jeans that showed her thong, then to her high-heeled Js that she'd thought were too hot to handle, then compared herself to the college girls who were fully dressed. Their beauty must've been on the inside, she guessed. Smart didn't come off a clothes rack.

"Let's go," she said to Gully. "I'm ready to go. I'm not feeling this lame scene."

He looked defeated, but nodded.

Before Santana could put the key in and turn the lock, someone from the other side of the door snatched it open. She paused for a moment, throwing a quick look behind her to Gully. He shrugged his shoulders.

"Surprise!" Meka yelled, jumping into sight.

Santana jumped up and down, then hugged her best friend she'd been missing. "When did you get out? How did you get out?"

Craig appeared with her mother by his side. He wore a big Kool-Aid smile.

Santana's mother patted his arm. "Your stepdad got her out. His firm's representing her—free of charge. What's that called again, baby?"

"Pro bono," he said, still smiling. "Surprise, step-daughter."

He's a lawyer? Santana had no idea. All this time she'd just thought of him as a man with money, not a man with a career.

Meka looped her arm through Santana's, then whispered in her ear. "We godda talk. That day I got locked

up, they let me out for a couple of days on my own rec-
ognizance—"

"Your own recogna-*who*?"

"Shh. Anyway, I went to that little getaway ya man
was having . . . and Nae was there. With him. With custom earrings on just like the ones he had designed for
you."

14

DYNASTY

She was going to be rich. Rich with a capital *R*, that's what City told her. Stretched out on his bed in Pork Chop's house, she believed him. There was money everywhere on the mattress. When she looked to her left, she came face to face with a dead president. When she turned to her right, she appreciated the Constitution even more. Moneyed men signed that American document, which gave her the right to many things, including earning her way out of the projects. And she appreciated them more and more every time she picked up a bill and saw one of their faces.

"Duck," City said, emptying a bag of money on her.

Dynasty laughed, rolling around in the greenbacks. She'd never had so much fun, except for the other night at the cabin party. She looked at City with new eyes, and hated that in her mind she'd reduced him to a common criminal.

"Word. I still can't believe you thought I was dealing!" He grinned, but she could feel his disappointment. "Talk about a case of the double *D*s—and not the breastesses *D*s either. I'm automatically a criminal because of the *D*s. I *dress* nice. *Drive* a nice car at an early age. And am *determined* to make it—legitimately. So, tell me again what you thought was in that bag. I have to hear it one more time." He sat down on the bed next to her, then laid back until his head was resting on her stomach.

She wanted to touch his hair. Tell him a whole bunch of other things, like how cute he was, how nice he was, how he made her feel as if she had a chance to make it too.

"I thought it was . . . drugs."

He laughed louder now. "Oh, it was drugs all right. Anything people are addicted to is considered a drug." He hit his fist in his hand, emphasizing his point. "But drugs though, Dynasty—I thought you had me figured better than that, kid."

"What did you expect? You said I was going to be distributing, and every boy in there who laid eyes on me and that bag, were open like they were—"

"On drugs! To them though, the autographed Lakers tickets, knockoff Rolexs, and T.O.P. and Trill's not-yet-released CDs are just that. All those dudes in there are window-dressing types. They care about how they look. They want people to think they went to the playoffs, sport ice, and have an in with the two hottest rappers of the south. But"—he turned his head and looked at her—"are you ready for what's next? The real money? The new addiction?"

She nodded. "Of course."

City sat up, then looked around the room. He punched his fist in his palm again. Then stood. "Okay, but you can't tell no one. This is a City and Dynasty exclusive."

She raised up on her elbows and watched him cross the room. He'd said his name and her name and exclusive in the same sentence, and that made her warm. She wasn't his girlfriend. He wasn't her guy. He just acted like they were together by coming around all the time, keeping her dressed with some money in her pocket, and encouraging her to excel academically. She watched him as he pushed his way inside the midsize closet, disappeared for a second, then appeared with a zippered garment bag.

"This is between us. I have your word on that?"

She loved his New York accent, his Brooklyn style. "Word."

He smiled, then unzipped the bag, and freed clothes from it. He laid each piece on the bed like a baby, very carefully. "What you think?"

Dynasty looked at the jeans, the button-down shirts, long and short sleeve, then glued her eyes to the tees. They were all hot—super hot, but she couldn't say she'd seen them before. "I like them. They're nice." She fingered the fabrics, then flipped over the jeans and saw rhinestones on them. "Rhinestones. Cool."

"No. Not rhinestones, crystals. Real one-hundred . . . and they're not just nice, Dynasty. They're our dinner. This is how we're going to eat and you're going to go to school."

She perked up now, pulling herself up until she could rest her butt back on her ankles. "What do you mean?"

A huge Kool-Aid smile spread on City's face. "This is

what I've been working on. I had an artist up north sketch out my ideas, sent that sketch to the next person, who turned them into patterns, then the patterns were sent to a sample maker. I took those samples—super high-end samples to a few people in the fashion and music biz, and voila. I got a couple rappers—namely, your boy Trill and his brother—are going to rock City Gear, my clothing line, in their next video and on the award shows."

She hopped up and wrapped her arms around his neck, held him, and rocked him. She was so proud of him that she almost kissed him, and certainly wanted to.

"So, this is the game plan. I'm going to keep getting the clothes made, and you can run the online store. You know, since you're so good with words, I figured you'd write the content . . . so the site don't look ghetto. I'm thinking, in the beginning, like the first year, you should be good for at least one-hundred-fifty a week, plus a City Gear wardrobe. In the second year, who knows? But we can definitely double it."

Dynasty's mouth opened. City made the money sound like nothing, but to her it was more than a start. Her brain kicked in. In the first year she could make almost eight stacks. The second year she could add almost sixteen to that. Who knew how much she could earn the third? But she did know one thing for certain; by the time college started she'd have a minimum of twenty-three thousand to help her begin her university life.

"You know something else?" City asked, looking deep into her eyes.

"What?"

"I like you, Dynasty. I like your style, your look, how you plan for the future. It's like we're the same person in two different bodies."

Dynasty blushed. She didn't realize that she had a *look*. Quickly, she gave herself a once-over. With nicer clothes, she had to admit that she wasn't bad on the eyes. She'd come a long way from being the skinny burnt-black poor girl Rufus had teased her about being. In fact, she looked at her dark complexion and City's, and finally realized that black was indeed beautiful and nothing to be ashamed about. She met City's stare again.

"I like you, too," she confessed, and felt something she'd never felt before. Love.

"I'm glad to hear that," said City, clapping his hands and pulling her out of a spell. "Now let's go get this money, honey."

Pork Chop had a third bedroom. An empty room next to City's that would serve as their office. A sign that read CITY GEAR INT. INC. was on the door, and two desks were inside, already set up with computers and other office materials. Large boxes were stacked in the corner, the closet, and some had smaller boxes on top of them. This was their inventory: clothing and accessories, some with rhinestones and others without. City had designed for the "average" consumer. The designs with real Australian crystals were in an old rifle safe that Pork Chop had bought years before. Upon inspection, Dynasty realized she could fit four of her in it.

"There's an instruction manual on your desk." City pointed. "We're going to first set up an eBay store, then roll out the real deal when the database and Web designers finish doing their part."

Dynasty sat in her office chair, fingering the leather armrests. Her life was changing, and she liked it. She guessed Aunt Maybelline had something to do with it; if she hadn't sent her on that mission impossible to get beer and cigarettes, Dynasty wouldn't have met City.

"Is it hard to do . . . the eBay thing, and inventory? Do I have to ship the merchandise too?" she questioned, loving how she'd moved right into business mode.

City walked over to her, then pulled her to her feet. He held both her hands. "For you, it's going to be easy. And I'll ship the goods twice a week. We should be ready after the trip to New York. . . ."

Her eyes brightened. He hadn't said anything about them going to New York.

"I only take my people home if they're special to me. Nah'mean? Can't take everyone home to your mother. And I thought you'd like to go, too, since we're fam now, and are going to build this business into a dynasty. So what's up? You down for next week? I can get Pork Chop to talk to your aunt."

Of course she wanted to go. "Yes!" She hugged him. "I'm ready."

He nodded, grabbing her hands again. Then looked at her as if he could finally see her. "There's something we need to get out of the way first. You never told me if you have a boyfriend. I'm sure someone has snatched you up by now."

"I've never really had a boyfriend. Friends maybe, but

nothing serious." She looked at his hands holding on to hers like he was afraid to let go. He had said that he was taking her to New York, and that he only took special people home to his mother, right? She grinned.

He reared back his head. "J.R.? Not even him? I thought something was up with you and him."

J.R. was a fool with feet. They'd hung out and he'd tried to kiss her, but she wouldn't let him because his breath smelled like smoke.

"We hung out, but that's it. There's someone I like though," she admitted again, and felt like a fool because she'd just told him minutes before that she liked him. Her nerves were getting to her.

City pulled her close, then wrapped his arms around her. He smelled as clean as he looked. "So no one has ever held you like this?"

She shook her head no. No one had, not even her mother, who'd traded Dynasty and her brother, King, for the streets and a life of drugs.

He lifted her chin, then looked into her eyes. "Anyone ever connect with you like this?"

Again, her head turned from side to side. Her stomach started to flutter, and her palms began to sweat. Her heart tried to beat its way out of her chest, and she couldn't make her lungs cooperate anymore; her breaths were sporadic, coming whenever and however they chose.

"So you've never been kissed either? I mean really kissed."

"Not really," she came clean. She'd been pecked on the lips, kissed on the cheek, and once some boy ran up to her as a dare, grabbed her face, and put his slobbery mouth on hers and tried to force his tongue into her mouth, but she refused to part her lips, and kicked him in his privates. So, no, she'd never been really kissed.

City bent forward, his hand still under her chin. "It's our job to look out for each other. You know that, don't you?"

She nodded.

"So since there's someone you *like*, I just can't have you going around not knowing what you're doing. Impressions are everything. And I think it's best that we get this out of the way so we can concentrate on business." Gently he put his lips on hers, giving her soft kisses. "We can't work together if it's too much tension. So do you mind if I *really* kiss you?"

She shook her head no again.

"Close your eyes," he instructed.

She did. Then she felt his mouth press against hers, and she parted her lips.

"Dynasty! Dynasty! Dynasty!" a woman's voice yelled from outside. "Come on out here!"

She ignored the voice for as long as she could, enjoying the kiss.

"Dynasty! Dynasty! Dynasty!" the voice repeated, not pausing between words.

City released her. "Who's that?"

"Lipstick. The woman who gave birth to me."

15

PATIENCE

It felt like someone was rubbing warm velvet across her eyelids. The soft texture and surrounding sweet scents sent a tingle up the back of her neck and tickled her head. Funky and stylish music, the kind she imagined Trill's stylist, Francoise, would listen to, filled the open space. She didn't know how the Make-up Art Cosmetics giant pulled off the exclusive feel of being a standalone makeup store in the middle of Macy's, but they did, and she loved it because she felt catered to.

"I used a touch of Shroom on the lids and under your brows to bring out your eyes," Emani, the makeup artist, said. "Under that, I used a Paint Pot to hold it in place."

"What about Fix Powder?" Silky asked.

Emani shook her head. "Child, no! Her skin—and yours, for that matter—doesn't need that much coverage. Utilize your youth for as long as you can."

Patience laughed at Emani's brashness, then scrolled through her messages on her cell. "Silky, look in my Hermés bag and pass me my iPad. Trill's in the studio and needs me to look up something."

Silky's hand went to her right hip, her neck moved to the left, and her brows shot toward the ceiling. "Your what? iPad? Hermés bag?" She reached for the oversized purse hanging from the chair Patience sat in, then flipped it over, reading the label. "I didn't know this was Hermés!" she exclaimed, pronouncing it just as it was spelled, not er-mez as it was properly pronounced. "And when did you get an iPad?" There was a hint of pride etched in her voice, but also a tinge of jealousy. "You doing big things now. . . ."

Patience grinned. "Thanks to you. You're the one that hooked me up. Trill's assistant-slash-publicist gave me the phone and iPad. His stylist, Francoise, hooked me up with the bag and trunks—and I do mean fashion trunks—of clothes. I'm sure he can get you a bag too. He works for a magazine sometimes, dressing models, so he has perks."

Silky relaxed and matched Patience's grin. "All right, look out for your BFF, BFF." She reached inside the bag and retrieved the sleek device. "So what do you have to look up?"

"Driving directions to the studio . . . for you," Patience informed, climbing down from the high makeup chair, flinging her hair over her shoulder, and checking out herself in the mirror. She was breathtaking, and felt like the stunner Trill always called her. She picked up the eight huge designer-store shopping bags that she'd acquired in less than two hours, and took the medium MAC bag from Emani.

Silky slid the iPad back into the purse, picked up her two Bebe bags, then danced in place. Though she only had a learner's permit, the Growler had given her driving privileges for the day so she could take Patience to the mall, and he'd thrown in some spending money for Silky as a courtesy—from Trill.

"Us got our hair did, nails did, face painted, and we's rocking them Robin's Jeans with five-inch low-platform stilettos, so we's ready," she sang, turning up her twang and laughing. "Let's do it! There's a GPS in the Range; we don't need the iPad."

"Wooo-weee," one of Trill's hangers-on said, then whistled when Patience entered the studio. He grimaced like he was in pain, holding the end of his balled fist up to his mouth and stomping his foot on the carpeted floor. "Day-um!" He stood up, then reached out his hand, giving Trill's brother a pound. "I godda go, partna. Ya baby bro's too protective of her, and she's looking so good and I'm so treed up, I can't help but look at her today. I don't wanna be disrespectin' homeboy, so I'm out." He walked toward Patience and Silky, looked Patience up and down, then shook his head. "Day-um!" he said, closing the door behind him.

Trill's brother looked at Patience and didn't acknowledge Silky. "What's up, Lil Sis? I see Teeny got you playing dress-up." He smiled. "You wear it well. You and my bruh's a good fit. He's in the booth. By the way, how's your crazy cousin Meka doing? Still strong-arming?"

"She's good. I haven't seen or talked to her because she got in a little trouble—that's what I heard Bishop telling my mom. But somehow she manages to text people like crazy."

" 'Cause she is crazy. She text *me*—and I didn't even give her my number. She said she's coming to collect her shoes when she get out, so I take it that them boys in blue got her. Shoplifting!" He laughed. "But you always need a crazy one on your team. 'Member that."

"Hiii, T," Silky sang to him. "I'm Silky, her best friend."

T just nodded at her, then turned toward the studio boards.

"Teeny?" Silky whispered to Patience. "I didn't know you knew her. When did you meet her? Where was I? And what's up with Meka? You introduced Meka to T, and not me?" She flopped down on the leather sofa looking defeated.

Patience sat next to her. "We needed Meka for a favor, and Teeny was at the after-party the night of the awards—the night you were supposed to meet me on the red carpet, remember? But you were too busy with your friend. Speaking of the Growler . . ." She nodded her head toward the door.

"What you doing here?" he growled at Silky.

"Wooo-weee," Trill exclaimed, pausing by the microphone booth's door. "Baby. Baby. Baby. I never thought . . ." he began, but couldn't finish. His eyes were so full of Patience's prettiness that he seemed to have forgotten his words.

T cleared his throat. "Man up, bruh."

Trill's expression changed from awe to laidback. "You . . . you . . ." He shook his head. "Man, lil momma. You stunning today. Never mind," he said, walking over and taking her hand. "T, gimme ten to clear my head before the next verse."

T licked his lips while his lean body bent over the boards, turning knobs and pressing buttons. "Nah, partna, bizness first—pleasure, I mean Patience, later. We still godda re-lay this hook 'cause the shawty who sung it, her voice don't match the track."

Trill reluctantly let Patience's hand go; then he went back into the booth, put a set of headphones on, and said through the microphone that he was ready. T pressed a button on the boards, and, like magic, the room filled with hypnotic beats. Patience and Silky smiled, nodding their heads to the music.

"That's hot," Silky said.

A girl's voice filled the air, singing catchy lyrics that the girls quickly caught on to. Silky hummed, and Patience sang along as quiet as she could.

"Lil Sis? Come over here," T said, calling Patience.

Patience pointed to her chest.

"Yeah, Lil Sis, you. Come on."

Patience rose from her seat and walked over to him. Her eyebrows were up and puzzlement covered her face.

"Sing that again. Louder this time. And—before you ask, yes, I'm talking to you," he said. He turned down the girl's voice and kept the music playing.

Patience closed her eyes and began. She was nervous, so she stumbled, then stopped. *I can do this,* she urged herself and relaxed. Moving her head to the music, she sang softly, then gained more confidence once she got the rhythm and lyrics down. Finally, as if the song were written by her, she belted out the words with a style all her own. A little R & B with just a touch of the hypnotizing gospel she'd learned to lace her choir voice with years ago made her sound infectious, and the whole studio caught on. For seconds, she became lost in the music and felt elevated. She forgot that she wasn't in the room alone, she didn't hear Trill come out of the microphone booth, and she didn't feel his presence next to her. The song ended. She opened her eyes. The people in the studio sat with their mouths open, then clapped like they were at a concert.

"Looks like we got a new, better singer for the hook," T said, smiling.

"Sure do!" Teeny said from the doorway. "I'll call and get a contract drawn up. Is that gonna be cool with your parents?"

"Yeah," Trill said, surprising Patience.

"That's my BFF! And there's always ways around signatures—like forgery," Silky said to the room. She stood up, pointing at her chest. "*My* BFF!"

Patience just nodded. She didn't know about signing her parents' signatures, but she was certain she wanted to work with Trill.

Trill looked at Patience with glazed eyes. "How 'bout that, lil Momma? You and me gonna make a record together."

"Nah," T said. "You and Lil Sis gone make history together. This here is a straight airwaves track—top-ten radio and billboards all the way, not underground. Go on and take that ten minutes, bro. Better yet, make it fifteen to match Lil Sis's first fifteen minutes of fame, and I do mean first. She ain't no hook singer—she's a straight-up full-album, going-on-the-road, Grammys singer."

His hand had taken hers before she knew it. They walked down the hallway of T's basement, where the studio was located, then up the stairs. A few more steps to the left, and they were outside. A bench was next to the lake in his yard, where a few ducks swam.

"So . . . you didn't tell me you could blow like that."

Patience smiled. "I told you I used to sing."

Trill grabbed her and pulled her close. "Yeah, but you didn't tell me you could sang—with an *A,* not an *I.* There's a difference between singin' and sangin'. Feel me?" He kissed her on her forehead.

Patience closed her eyes, then stiffened. She'd forgotten she was Bishop's daughter for a second, but now she remembered.

"The Bishop's not going to allow me to sing on your song. There's no way . . ."

"There's godda be a way. You and me—together, we'll come up with something. Singing is your gift."

"Gift" awakened something in Patience. A new energy and assuredness surged through her like a live wire. "You know what, Trill? You're right. It is my gift—not Bishop's. God gave that gift to me so I can use it." She pursed her lips, remembering one of her father's sermons. He'd preached that it'd be a sin not to use what God gave us to use—that it's like a slap in the face to turn away the gifts of the Father. But he never stated that all gifts were to be used religiously. God didn't discriminate, so why should she? Patience questioned.

"Baby, I'm going to go in there and sing—I mean, sang—on that track, and we'll just have to come up with me a stage name."

A smile spread on Trill's face. "That's my girl. You are my girl, right?"

Patience nodded. "You asking me? Or just checking to be sure?"

Trill bent down to kiss her, and Patience's phone went off. He took it out of her hand, then made a face. "That's your sister texting you. Said your parents are coming home in a couple of hours, so I guess you godda go . . . unless . . . I want you to stay with me. My house is full of people, but T and Teeny are leaving tonight. . . . It'll be just me here."

Patience felt bad. She knew she couldn't stay, and she would've been afraid to even if she could. She was a virgin and would remain one until she married. She wasn't in a rush to be too grown. She had plans for her future, including two college degrees that she'd get no matter what or how many albums T predicted were in her future. She shrugged, then shook her head no.

"Not if you ever want to see me again—or perform with you at any shows." She sounded like she was joking, but really she was serious. "I can go in there and sing the hook now, but if we want a future together, we're going to have to come up with a plan. You can wait for me, right?"

Trill bit his lip. "Yeah," his mouth uttered, but his expression said something else. "Let's go lay your vocals real quick. I think you should be able to do it in under an hour. That'll give you enough time to get home before your father gets in."

Patience didn't like the look on his face, and it scared her. She didn't want to lose him, not when she was just finding herself. "How about this? I lay the vocals, go home, then meet you back here at midnight? But you have to get me back before five in the morning."

Trill smiled. "Yeah!"

The house was dark when Silky pulled into the drive, and her sister's car was gone. Patience threw her jeans and shirt and stilettos in the backseat, and continued to scrub her face with disposable makeup-remover moist wipes. She'd changed her clothes and been taking off her makeup on the ride home. "All clean?"

Silky nodded. "Yes. Now hurry up and get in there before he gets home. I'll bring your bags and clothes to you tomorrow."

Patience hopped out of the borrowed Range Rover, slipping back on her good-girl ballerina flats. She shut the door and waved bye to Silky. Giving the house the once-over, she relaxed a bit. Her sisters had left, but all was still clear. Bishop's and her mother's cars weren't in front of the house in the circular drive like usual. She looked at her watch, and saw she was forty minutes early.

"Whew," she said, unlocking the door and walking inside. She headed straight for the steps, and ran up to her room.

There he was. Bishop. He sat on her bed, holding her

Louis Vuitton bag and sunglasses, and something else. A remote control. He clicked on her TV. "I want you to see something." He selected RECORDED SHOWS, scrolled to one, and pressed PLAY.

Patience's jaw dropped. There she was. On TV. She was on the red carpet, her arm wrapped around Trill's as he told the world to get used to seeing them together because he was trying to make her his girlfriend.

"So you're a keeper now?" Bishop boomed. "On television, dressed up like a floozy, with a street thug! Well, I'll tell you what, Patience. The only thing worth keeping around here is The Good Book. So you're going to keep it for months—months. Let's see if your thug thinks you're worth keeping after he hasn't seen you for months. The only thing you're going to be doing is studying, going to church, and studying some more. I'll make sure of that! Why oh why did your mother have to be at the women's retreat?" he asked no one, surely wanting someone else to do what he refused to do—parent his daughter. He got up slowly, taking her purse and sunglasses with him, and walked to her door. "Now turn to the book of Exodus and commit to memory the Fifth Commandment about honoring your father and mother."

Patience froze. She was hurt, enraged, and disgusted. She didn't know how Bishop found out about the awards, but she'd get to the bottom of it. And if her sisters turned out to be snitches, she didn't know what she'd do to them, but it would be something they'd regret. Deeply. She cringed, and, suddenly, gospel music filled the house. That meant Bishop had retired to his office to study or meditate; that's what he always did when he was mad, to prevent "lowering" himself to worldly men's ways—physically hurting his girls. Patience pulled out her cell phone from her pocket, ran inside her closet, and called Trill.

The sound of her voice singing met her ears from the other line. The hook she'd laid vocals on sounded even better. "Hello?"

"This is Trill's phone," a female voice finally answered.

Whew! Teeny would know what to do, Patience believed. "I see you're listening to the song. I think I did a pretty good job on the hook. It sounds good, right, Teeny?"

"Hmm. Your vocals? Did you just say *your vocals?*"

"Yes!" Patience whispered, full of excitement. "T had me lay them earlier, Teeny. I was afraid, but—"

"This ain't Teeny. She's out of town."

"Well, who's this?" Patience asked.

"*Who* is this? Don't be calling asking me who I am. You the one calling," the girl snapped.

"This is Trill's girlfriend," Patience shot back.

"Well, *Trill's girlfriend*," the girl mocked, laughing. "He's busy now . . . and you had the right idea earlier about being afraid. Trust me, you should still be afraid. Very afraid of losing your man."

Patience hung up the phone and cried. She guessed he couldn't wait for her after all.

16

SANTANA

There were uniforms everywhere. Every. Where. Pleated plaid skirts, white button-down shirts, and shoes on top of shoes, on top of shoes. Santana stole glances at the girls' feet, and came to a conclusion. Since they couldn't dress how they wanted, they went hard in the kicks department. Ultra cement-hard. Stripper-high strappy sandals. Killer Louboutins. Pairs and pairs of some she couldn't recognize, but all were fire hot. But no one, she beamed with pride, rocked Js like she did. They were so behind, she thought as she held her head high and strutted down the hallway with her Gucci bag on her shoulder, then looked around, realizing she had no idea where she was going.

"Lost?" a freckle-faced girl asked, wearing a smile. She had a HALL MONITOR badge proudly pinned to her shirt.

Santana pursed her lips, then threw her color-crayon-red waist-length weave over her shoulder. "Uh. *Yay-yah!*

Ain't we all . . . since we all holed up in dis school during summa."

The girl's smile faded and her jaw fell. Then she raised her eyebrows and crossed her arms. She burst out laughing. "Are you *serious*?"

Santana didn't catch the joke. Mirroring the girl, she crossed her arms, then snaked her neck. "Uh *yay-yah*!" If she'd been chewing gum, now would've been the perfect time to pop it, she thought while she checked her phone, that had finally been returned, for a text message from Meka.

The girl turned up her laughter and doubled over, snatching Santana's attention back. When she rose, tears were welled in her eyes.

"What's so funny, Kenzy?" another girl with skin the color of Santana's and shoes many would die for, asked, making her way over.

Kenzy, the one who was in stitches, pointed to Santana. "Ask her—I'm sorry, what's your name?" she managed between fits of laughing.

Santana looked from Kenzy to the black girl. "Santana," she said dryly. "And I still don't know what's so funny."

"I'm Chase," the girl with the funky shoes offered.

"Santana, please tell Chase what you said to me!" Kenzy gathered herself, then eyed Chase.

"I said, 'Uh. *Yay-yah!* Ain't we all lost . . . since we all holed up in dis school during dis hot summa.'"

"Oh gawd!" Chase doubled over in laughter too, with Kenzy parroting her. "Santana, you are *too* fun-nee. What were you watching? What comedian are you mimicking?! *Who* talks like that? Oh gawd, Kenzy, have you ever heard something so fun-nee before? Must've been an old Martin Lawrence show on television. I love how you've incorporated what's-her-name's ghetto-girl mentality . . . Shanaynay, into your look today . . . and that knockoff bag. What a way to break the ice at a new school!" Tears sprang from her eyes as she fingered Santana's color-crayon-red weave and eyed her high-heeled Js. "Michael Jordan had nothing to do with that shoe design! Trust me."

Me. Santana crumbled inside. *Me. That's how I talk.* The girls were serious and laughing at her and didn't know it. *What's wrong with the way I speak? My hair? My Js!* she wondered. They were the different ones, not her. They were lame, squares who didn't fit in the round world . . . weren't they? *Yes.* If they were in her old neighborhood, in her previous school, in the life she'd had until recently, they'd be clowned, and their tears wouldn't be from laughing.

"Welcome to Winchester Hills Prep!" Chase said, giving her air kisses on both cheeks. "We need someone here with your lively and fun-nee take on life."

I'm in their world, Santana realized, hating it more and more with each passing second. She didn't have time for this—not today. In one hour she was supposed to meet Meka outside so she could get the digs on Pharaoh, slide up on him while he wasn't looking, and then rock his world as he knew it. He'd been ducking her, dodging her calls, and missing in action. She knew why, and she'd get to the bottom of it, even if it meant dragging Nae down the street.

"Thanks . . . I guess," Santana returned Chase's greeting. "But on the real, dough, y'all need to get on top of dis. Stop acting all Erica Kane and snap to reality," she set them straight. "Wait. I'm gonna show y'all how we do on the other side. Friday's casual dress-how-you-are day, right? Watch how I turn up the heat with my 'fit then!" she said, slashing outfit in half.

"Word! We can't wait to see what you pull next!" Chase said without the least bit of sarcasm or tease in her voice. Then she and Kenzy walked down the hall holding each other up, laughing like two wild hyenas.

Meka's borrowed vehicle was sitting exactly where she said it'd be. Santana strolled carefully, glancing behind her every now and then to make sure she wasn't being followed. She'd been warned that the school frowned upon skipping classes and cutting out early, but she didn't care. Life went on, and so would school—tomorrow. Today was reserved for Pharaoh.

"Hop in!" Meka yelled, pushing open the door. "There's some dude dressed in the blues with a rent-a-cop badge on."

Santana ran to the car and hopped in. "Go! Go! Floor this mug."

Meka took her time strapping herself in. She turned on the system, found the hip-hop station, and adjusted the volume.

"Meka? What, are you trying to get me in trouble?"

Meka laughed. "Girl, you're already changing. There's no security following you. I was only playing. Dang." She purred the engine, threw the car in drive, then skidded off like she raced for NASCAR. "I still don't get what you all bent outta shape for. You know what it is with Pharaoh now, so maybe you should just move on. Maybe you can come with me to New York, get your mind off of that lame you call a boyfriend."

Santana side-eyed her friend. "Move on? What, you on Nae's side now? This is about principle, Meka. And you know I'm in year-round school now, so I can't hop a plane and go anywhere. And who wants to be third-wheel?"

"Mm-hm," Meka said, rounding a corner. "We'll see about principle!" She turned up the music until Santana couldn't hear herself think, and they drove the rest of the way in silence.

The block was exceptionally crowded when Meka weaved the car through the throngs of people and cars in the middle and on the sides of the street. A WELCOME HOME banner was stretched across someone's porch, telling Santana the occasion. Someone had just come home from jail. From the looks of things—the two DJs, four barbecue grills, numerous spades and dice games—whoever it was had been gone pretty long. The neighborhood only went all out like this for people who'd taken a ten-year-or-more stretch behind bars.

"Must be an old head, 'cause we ain't heard about them coming home. I'll say this, whoever he or she is did a long bid. . . ." Meka said, letting her words marinate. "Maybe Federal . . . ooh, over there." Meka pointed.

There sat Pharaoh's car with him leaned up against it. A crowd of dudes stood around him, clearly engaged by whatever he was saying or doing.

Santana jumped out of Meka's ride before she could kill the engine. She was furious, happy and excited all at once. Her legs carried her to him in long strides, and she was almost running. But jogging to a man was just something you didn't do, not when you were the hottest thing to ever grace the streets of the ATL.

"Where ya been?" she cut into him before she reached him.

"Er'where, shawty. Where you been?" He cracked a smile and stretched his arms wide. "Don't be walking up on me questioning me, and don't bring ya boy no love."

Santana grabbed him by his arm, pulling him away from his car and his boys. "I godda talk to you. Now."

Pharaoh pulled away from her as smooth and cool as he could. She knew he wouldn't want anyone to see her yoking him up, but she didn't care.

"Look, shawty. I know yo moms put you on lock down, but you ain't been gone long enough to forget who the man around here is. Don't be snatching on my clothes."

Santana put her hand on her hip. "Well, who can snatch on your clothes—or should I say snatch off your clothes? Nae? Your other girl who you bought earrings like mine for?"

He threw his head back, then looked down at her. He bit his bottom lip, showing off his grills. "Come on now, shawty. Nae went to the same store and had them make some like yours. What you talking 'bout?"

"I heard Nae was with you at the cabin. Is that true?" Santana snapped.

"Lots of people was there."

"Were you with Nae? Don't make me havta ask you again." Cars sped by and people walked around them and barbecue smoke filled the air, but there was still no response from Pharaoh. "You hear me?"

"Santana!" Meka's voice cut through the one-sided argument Santana was having.

"I said do you hear me?"

"Look, shawty, you my girl—not my moms. Don't be raising your voice—"

"San. Tan. Ah!" Meka's voice bellowed, cutting off Pharaoh.

"*What?*" Santana snapped back, looking across the street at Meka.

Meka pointed to her phone, mouthing *Look at yours.*

Santana took her cell out of her purse, and saw the text.

UR PARENTS NO U CUT SKOOL. DEY ON DEY WAY HERE. MEET GULLY AROUND DA CORNER N DA BACK OF DA GAS STATION SO HE CAN TAKE U HOME. IF DEY SEE ME & PHARAOH HERE, YOU CAN GET OUTTA TROUBLE. GODDA SCOOP MY NEW LOUBOUTINS FROM MY CUZ PATIENCE. CALL U L8TR.

"What's good, shawty? Why you look so grim?" Pharaoh asked.

Santana just shook her head. "I godda go. Look, I'm tired of chasing you, so if you want to be with Nae, do you."

Pharaoh pulled Santana to him, then kissed her on her

forehead. "I don't want her. I just been busy, the boys in blue been bringing down heat on ya boy, and I didn't want you to get caught up. Okay, shawty? We'll talk about Nae later. She was there, but it wasn't nothing. Trust me."

Santana pulled away from him, then cut through a few backyards, making her way to the gas station. She wanted to finish the conversation, get down to the truth, but she couldn't risk her freedom again, not after just getting off of punishment.

"Hurry, Santana!" Gulliver waved her over. "If we get you back up to the school quickly, you can go into the nurse's office and complain about female problems. Say you were in the bathroom or something."

Santana looked at Gulliver with new eyes. He was more than all right with her. He was her friend, and she knew she could trust him. That was more than she could say for Pharaoh.

17

DYNASTY

Lipstick was a mess. A real live wire of a mess that was in Dynasty's way, her personal business, clothes that City had bought her, and was now taking up room on her mattress. She lay there, looking up at the ceiling, and trying to see how far her smoke rings would rise. She coughed, and it sounded as if a garbage truck were stuck in her throat, rumbling. She reached over to the floor, grabbed her tube of lipstick, and painted her lips with it over and over. Dynasty sat on a chair in front of the window watching her and wondered how on earth did someone put on lipstick and smoke at the same time. Her mother had her own technique. She'd hold the cancer stick between her lips and work the waxy color around it, only burning her hand once or twice a day, which wasn't a lot since she applied the makeup every fifteen minutes or so.

"So you still mad?" she had the nerve to ask Dynasty.

Dynasty just looked at her. What made her mother think that pale orange, bright fuchsia, or silver lipstick went with a dark complexion? Her lips rotated among looking like someone had dyed them the same color as potent urine, looking like they'd been dipped in fluorescent pink paint, and looking like they'd been dusted with flour. *She's color blind.* She watched as her mom changed her mind, wiping off the orange, then applied a color Dynasty hadn't noticed before today. Lavender. *Great!*

"I know you hear me, Dynasty. What, you mad cause you can't go to New York?"

No, I'm mad because you show up and want to pretend to be a mother, then disappear.

"When are you going to rehab?" asked Dynasty, cracking open her dictionary. She figured she might as well learn something new while listening to her mother lie, because that's what was coming next.

Lipstick pushed her almost-one-hundred-pound body up from lying on the mattress, then turned sideways and kicked out her bare feet. Her toes were crusty and her soles looked like they'd been walking through cooling coals. Her hair stood wildly on top of her head, and was different lengths. It looked like rats had been sucking on it. She shook a little and nodded. Dynasty could tell her mom was high. The nod gave her away.

"I'm thinking about going next week. But—" She licked her lips, plucked nonexistent lint from her flimsy tank top that covered her flat, saggy, braless breasts. "But . . ." Her eyes rolled up into her head. "Whew!" She rubbed her chin and continued licking the lavender from her lips.

"Your mouth dry, too?" she asked, managing to open her eyes.

"When, Lipstick? When are you going to rehab?"

Lipstick banged one ashen foot on the floor. "When I feel like it! Don't be asking me no stupid questions. I'm yo momma. I ask you."

Dynasty turned and looked out the window, then stood and stuck her head out. From where she was, she could see City putting his luggage in his trunk. She turned back, saw her piece of a mother suffocating her teenage life, and she wanted more than ever to go with City. The trip was only going to be a couple of days, and she'd explained it to her mother. Told her how it'd be good for her education, earning money, and saving for college, but Lipstick didn't care. She'd told Dynasty that she was a child, and as her mother, it was up to Lipstick to make the rules. It took every ounce of strength that Dynasty had to stop her from telling Lipstick that she didn't have a mother. But the truth was she didn't. Not since she was one year old.

The bedroom door burst open, and Aunt Maybelline appeared in her classic clownishness. Drawn-on eyebrows. Inch-long eyelashes thickly coated with crusted mascara. More eyeliner than the law should allow and circles of orange creamy blush on her cheeks were only outdone by the cherry-red lipstick that bled past her lip line, clearly mirroring Lipstick's, and her wig was matted and tilted to one side. Aunt Maybelline stood there in a cloud of smoke. Dynasty shook her head. *Now I live with Bozo and Ronald McDonald.*

"Lipstick! Lipstick! Get up!" Aunt Maybelline yelled as if she weren't right in front of them. "You ate my last doggone pork chops! Yeah, heifer, Pork Chop told me. And he said you was scheming on my green jelly shoes, my good wig, and my medications."

Lipstick managed to lift her head, though it still bobbed. She laughed. "Heifer, you crazy. Ain't nobody eat Pork Chop! How I'm gonna eat your man?"

"Come on!" Maybelline invited. "Come get this whoopin'."

Dynasty stood up to leave. There was no way she was going to watch this madness. A drunk crazy person and a heroin addict fighting wasn't her idea of entertaining. It was sad, and she just hated that it was a part of her life. She skirted her thin frame around Aunt Maybelline's heft and smoke, zipped through the hallway, down the steps, and out the door as fast as she could. If she was lucky, she'd be able to catch City. And if she did, she'd beg him to take her with him.

"Shuckey duckey, quack, quack. Unlucky, hungry-looking, and burnt black. What's going on, Die Nasty?" called Rufus from his throne, the grungy picnic table bench, while his hand was stuck in a bag of potato chips. A bottle of hot sauce was on the table, and from the red saucy stains dripping down his shirt, it was apparent that he'd been using it. He put the bag of chips to his mouth, then dusted off the contents, then swapped it for a super-large bag of pork skins.

Dynasty crossed her arms over her shoulders and

shook her head. She'd maneuvered the projects once and, now, almost twice, but City's car was nowhere to be found. She couldn't believe her luck. She'd only seen him loading his things into the trunk a couple of minutes before she'd bolted down the steps and out of the apartment.

"Please, not today, Rufus . . . okay?"

Rufus got up from the bench and laid the pork skins on the table. He wiped crumbs from his mouth, and tried to dust the chips and crackled pig skin from his hands as he walked over to her. He tilted his head and eyed her like a science project.

"Please?" he almost whispered. "You okay, Dynasty?" he questioned softly. "You know I tease you a lot, and I know you think I'm a troublemaker, but that's only because you're my friend."

"I know, Rufus. . . ." She stared down the parking lot, past the other parked cars, hoping for a sign of City. She didn't feel them at first, and wished they'd dry up and disappear, but she couldn't stop them. The tears came naturally, but they weren't cleansing.

"You crying? Why you crying?" Rufus stooped down until his face was in front of hers. "Dynasty, please don't cry. I ain't never seen you cry. You the strongest person I know."

Dynasty leaned into Rufus. Her arms were still crossed. Her tears kept flowing. Her shoulders moved up and down as she began to heave. She felt as if someone— Lipstick—had reappeared in her life to ruin her world. She hated her mother. Well, not her mother, but the drug addict who'd moved into her mom's body, and made her ruin everything and hurt her children. City was her only way out for now; he'd taken better care of her in the past weeks than Lipstick had in her whole life. He didn't make her feel like a check like Aunt Maybelline, and he hadn't tried to take her innocence or lied on her like J.R. More important, he was her friend, and though he was all boy, he'd become her cheerleader, pushing her to do better and celebrating her accomplishments and the new words she added to her vocabulary. She wasn't supposed to be here; she was supposed to be in New York. Now Lipstick had messed that up too. Why couldn't she just go away?

Rufus kissed the top of her head. "You know what, Dynasty. Im'a hurt 'em. Whoever made you cry is dead meat. Don't nobody mess with my friend and get away with it."

Dynasty looked up and saw that Rufus was serious. Upset about not being able to go with City, she'd forgotten that Rufus was her friend too. He got on her nerves, played too much, and called her all kinds of names, but he was always there. Had been for years.

"Thanks, Dufus," she said, smiling and wiping away her tears.

"No problem, burnt-black crybaby." He let her go, then resumed his position back on the picnic-table bench. The plastic bag crunched when he picked it up. He looked at the pork skins like they were gold, then moved his stare on Dynasty. He shrugged like he was trying to make a decision. "'Ey? You a bookworm, so answer this question for me 'cause you know I don't know all the words like you do. But maybe one day you could help me . . . ? You know, so people can stop calling me stupid."

Her heart fell. She'd called him stupid more times than she could count, but she never meant it. She hoped he knew that. "Sure, I'll help you. What do you want to know."

"What's it called when someone offers you something so y'all can make up? There's a word for that, right?"

"A peace offering."

He held the bag her way. His peace offering. "Have some?"

Dynasty crossed her eyes and stuck out her tongue. "Rufus, you trying to make up with me? You're extending *me* a peace offering?" She couldn't believe it.

Rufus snatched back the bag, then looked away from her. She could tell he was embarrassed. "No, Dynasty. Ain't nobody trying to be your friend!"

"Thank you, Rufus," she said, smiling. She turned around, deciding it was time to get back to the house. As much as she couldn't stand to be around an addict, she wasn't sure how long it'd be before her mother disappeared again. That's how she'd started to view Lipstick, as two people: the addict, and the woman who gave birth to her.

" 'Welcome, burnt-black. I'll check you later."

Dynasty set down the college dictionary, then picked up an unabridged one. She'd been in her room for hours thumbing through pages, searching for just the right words for Rufus. Before she could open the heavy book, Aunt Maybelline felt the need to disrupt her life. She'd just put her hands on the old dust cover, wanting to lose herself in the prized words and come up with a list that'd make Rufus feel better. Good words that he could learn and grasp.

"Dynasty! Get yo behind down here."

She could hear the slur in her aunt's voice and smell the puff of smoke that she was sure was lingering around her head in a cloud before she made it back down the steps. She cradled the dictionary to her side.

"Ma'am?"

"That big black boy that you be with. The one who be scheming on my shoes . . ." she began, then pulled on her cigarette.

"You mean Rufus."

"Yeah. Him. One of his sorry, equally big and black little snot-nosed brothers just came here and said he fell out. Had a heart trouble or something. Oh, yeah . . ." Aunt Maybelline added before Dynasty made it through the front door. "Lipstick done took off again . . . and she took my pork chops."

There was an oxygen mask on Rufus's face and what seemed like hundreds of white sticky circles with wires coming out of them stuck to his chest. Dynasty's eyes followed the wires to a heart monitor, where wavy lines moved across the screen. His heart was working, but she couldn't tell if it was beating hard enough or too hard.

"Sorry, Rufus. I'm sorry for not always being nice to you." She put her head on the hospital-bed bar.

"You should be sorry," Rufus remarked, surprising her.

She sat up and smiled. "You okay?"

Rufus attempted to smile back. "I am now. 'Least now I know you're really my friend and don't just feel sorry for me. My only friend."

Dynasty picked up the dictionary and began reading words to Rufus. Words like *confidant*, *ally*, and *steadfast*. Words that described Rufus.

18

PATIENCE

Her shoes. Patience had searched mountain high and gutter low, and still hadn't been able to find the shoes Trill had bought her. And, after Bishop sat on her bed holding her purse and sunglasses, he'd kept his promise about punishing her and made sure she had plenty of time to hunt for anything she wanted to find. Plenty. She'd been locked down for two weeks, and during that time had scoured her room and closet, then made rounds throughout the house, starting with both of her sisters' bedrooms. She'd come up empty handed each time. Still though, she was determined. She may've been upset with Trill in the beginning, but she still wanted to wear his gift. She exhaled, thinking about him and that crooked smile she loved so much. Even though she wasn't completely over the girl at the studio, the mean heifer who threatened her, she missed him. At first her anger had been something bordering on hate, but as the days added up and he'd called, e-mailed, and texted her more times than she could count, her attitude calmed. Especially once she discovered the girl was the one she replaced on the track.

"She's just jealous," Patience told herself, turning back on the vacuum cleaner.

She'd been sentenced to hard time. Too hard and too much, she thought, calculating how many more rows and pews she'd have to clean in the church. Bishop had instructed the cleaning crew that Patience was responsible for one of the balcony sections, and that was a lot of space to clean in a mega, stadium-sized church. Her phone vibrated in her pocket, and she smiled. It had to be Trill because Silky had gone back overseas to tour with her mother. Because she had no idea if Bishop was watching her on the cameras, she kept on vacuuming, and decided to call Trill back later from one of the places she knew Bishop didn't monitor, the women's bathrooms.

All the lights switched off, and Patience rolled her eyes. Who'd shut them off at this time of day when so much had to be done? she wondered. Suddenly, as quick as they had shut off, the lights in the lower section came back on. From where she stood, she could see the stage was lit. A live sax blew, then melodic music she'd never heard before filled the space. Patience closed her lids, moved by the sounds. Despite what The Good Bishop believed, gospel music was intoxicating too, just like Trill's raps and Silky's mother's songs. So how could anything so moving, so elevating, be considered bad?

A voice like none she'd ever heard before sang to her from below. Patience closed her eyes again. The beautiful alto caressed her ears and seemed to erase her anger caused by the Bishop and the hurt she felt over not being able to see Trill. The voice switched to tenor, then bass, then somehow did the unthinkable—it flipped back into alto again. She never would've guessed it was possible. Sure, she'd heard of people being able to master a couple ranges, but not three. *Four?* she questioned when a smooth soprano met her ears. Her lids shot open and tears streamed down her face. No one had ever made her cry before, not from singing. In a rush, she dropped the vacuum handle and made her way down to the first row of the balcony. She had to see whom the voice belonged to. She was only able to see his back, and it wasn't enough.

In a flash, she zoomed up the balcony steps, pushed her way through the door, and took off down the stairs that led to the main floor, almost falling once or twice. She didn't care. The only thing that mattered to her was getting to the owner of the voice.

"If this is what Bishop means by being moved by the spirit, well, let it move me faster then!" she said, as she barged through the heavy double doors that led to the sanctuary, then froze. In her rush, she hadn't realized how much noise she was making or how much strength she had until the doors ricocheted off the walls, banging like bombs and causing the singer and sax player to stop. "Sorry," was all she could say.

"Hello," the boy greeted from afar.

Patience's eyes stretched. She hadn't realized the owner of the voice belonged to someone so young. From where she stood, she could tell he wasn't Trill. He looked ordinary, maybe even a little square. She laughed. He looked like she did only weeks ago, and here she was judging him.

In hard-bottom loafers, jeans, and a shirt that was buttoned all the way up, he made his way over to her. Up close, she thought he looked like he was choking, and she wanted to reach up, loosen a button or two, and free his neck. She didn't want anything to restrict his breathing; he'd need his breath to sing.

"Hi . . ." she managed to answer, staring at him. He seemed familiar, but she couldn't think of where she'd seen him before. She was certain she hadn't run into him at church. She'd remember him if she had.

The boy reached over, and swiped his warm hand across her face. "You okay?"

"Yes. Why would you ask—"

"Then why are you crying?" He was concerned as if he knew her.

The old Patience—the Patience before Trill—would've told him that he and that beautiful voice brought her to tears, but that wasn't her anymore. *Man up*, she urged herself.

"I'm good." It wasn't a lie; she was great now because he'd erased her troubles and pushed Trill to the back of her mind. "I'm—"

"Patience. I know. Bishop said you'd be here taking care of some important church business. I hope I'm not disturbing you." He smiled, and she could see he was genuine.

He doesn't know I'm on punishment. Good. She took a closer look at him, and realized that he was no Trill.

But he didn't have to be. He had a church-boy-next-door appeal to him that said he could be trusted and she felt as if she knew him. His cocoa skin and deep dimples also showed promise. If only she could talk him into getting rid of that army box cut some barber had butchered his head with, he'd be someone she could be seen with. *Wait a minute.* What was she thinking? She had a boyfriend. Or did she? she questioned. After the "talk" with the girl at the studio, she wasn't so sure. Even though Trill had assured her the girl wasn't there for him and had just un-expectedly showed up to re-lay her vocals, which of course she couldn't do thanks to Patience's taking the song, a warning in Patience's gut said something else. In-stinct told her that she hadn't only taken the girl's vocals but maybe, just maybe, also the girl's boyfriend—Trill. *Were they together?*

She shook away her insecurities and doubts, remem-bering the voice.

"No, you didn't disturb me. In fact, you saved me . . . from overworking."

He smiled. "You have time for a little more saving? I forgot my earpiece and can't fully hear myself without it. Do you mind?"

Earpiece? Was he hard of hearing?

"Mind what?"

"Telling me how I sound. I'm practicing for something very important. And . . . you know, without being able to hear what I sound like to the audience . . . it's just weird."

Patience leaned against the pew, wondering how to ask

him if he had a hearing problem. "But you can hear me just fine—"

He laughed. "Not a hearing aid, an earpiece—technically it's called an in-ear monitor. You know, like a mic for your ears so you can hear your range, what you sound like to the audience. I'm sure you've seen them in singer's ears before while they were performing."

Ahh. Now she understood. Patience laughed too, leaning forward to touch him while she did. "I'm just playing. I just wanted to see if you would fall for it."

He nodded, walking back toward the stage. "Yeah, okay. If you say so. How about you be my in-ear piece, then afterwards we go to lunch so you can tell me what you think? My treat."

Patience walked next to Choir Boy as he strolled through the parking lot toward an exit. She hadn't traveled by foot in so long it almost felt foreign. At a loss for words, she sized him up. He was shorter than Trill, a little thicker, and his jeans, which stopped just at the bottom of his ankles, had a slick gleam to them. *Over pressed, over starched.* He did—thank God—have on trouser socks, and not white ones like she'd assumed he would. Still though, he bordered on average. Bordered because he wasn't regular, he was stuck somewhere in the middle of normal and square. She shook her head. Poor thing.

"So . . ." she decided to break the silence, but didn't know his name. She'd assigned him a nickname like she did everyone, a trait she'd inherited from her father. Trill had been Pretty Boy. Silky's boyfriend was the Growler. Now the nice guy with the pretty voice was Choir Boy.

"So . . ." he answered back. "Tell me about Patience."

She began to point at her chest, then stopped herself, thinking of T. *Yeah, he's talking to me.* "What do you want to know?"

They exited the lot and turned right, and she wondered where they were going. Nothing was close. All the restaurants, dives, and stores were at least four or five blocks away, country miles as her mother called them. The church grounds were enormous, so they'd have to walk past the business offices, homeless center, and public works where all the machinery and extra equipment was housed.

"I want to know about Patience. What do you like to do? What school do you go to? How old are you? What's your passion?" he drilled her. "Not in that order. Just tell me something."

Patience reeled her head back and stopped. She assumed he knew more than he led her to believe. He did, after all, say Bishop told him about her.

"You wanna know why I was in the church today, is that what you're asking?"

Choir Boy laughed. "No. Why would I ask that? The question is, why wouldn't you be in church? Why wouldn't everyone want to be in their place of refuge?"

Now she knew he was crazy. He sounded just like Bishop, and she told him so. "I guess when you grow up, you're going to go to theology school, then Seminary, and minister to the world and save it too, huh? I guess when you grow up you're not going to live and have fun and go out and dance and listen to secular music. You'll probably shield your family from the world until all they seek is the world because you're going to be too busy saving everyone else that you forget about the ones under your roof," Patience lashed out.

Choir Boy whistled. "I take it you're mad at your father for his calling? Don't answer that. I shouldn't have said that." He put his hands on Patience's shoulders. "When I grow up, I'm going to do me. I'm going to live how I want to live like I do now. And believe it or not, I go out. I listen to all kinds of music. I even dance. I'm not a dancer, I'm terrible at it, but I do it. Believe it or not, I even date," he teased, raising his eyebrows and flirting. "In fact, I'm preparing for prom—already lining up all of my girls to see which one's going to match my tux!"

They both laughed.

"Enough of this seriousness. I want some ice cream, a milkshake, something cold and frosty." He began walking.

Patience caught up to him, and drew her eyebrows together. "Won't that be bad on your throat? Dairy? You said you're preparing for something big. You know dairy's not good for you now. What are you preparing for anyway?"

"Ahh. Bishop did mention that one of his daughters used to sing. Must've been you. Who knows, Patience, maybe we'll sing a duet together."

They turned the corner. With each step she tried to figure out why he seemed familiar, but she wouldn't ask him. She liked how their conversation was flowing, and she didn't want to stop it.

"I didn't used to do anything. I still sing, thank you very much. You didn't answer my question."

He grabbed her hand, and she started to pull away, but stopped herself. His touching her was friendly. Brotherly even.

"The Stellar Awards."

"*The* Stellar Awards. The gospel equivalent of the Grammys . . . good for you, Choir Boy." Her nickname for him fled her mouth before she could stop it.

"Look at you, all flirting with me and stuff, and you don't even know my name. If I didn't know any better, I'd think you were trying to match my tux for prom."

They rounded another corner, and the main street was in sight.

"Okay, you got me. What is your name, Choir Boy?"

He smiled. "Tell me your boyfriend's name first, then I'll tell you."

"Trill," she admitted before she knew it. "Man . . . please don't tell Bishop."

The smile from Choir Boy's face faded. "Trill? As in the award-winning, doughboy who all the ladies love more than Cool J, Trill?"

Patience nodded, and though she tried not to rub it in Choir Boy's face, she smiled. "Sorry."

He raised his brows and looked down the street. "There's a DQ down there. Ice cream! And there's no need to be sorry—not yet. If anything, I should be sorry, because Trill is definitely competition. He's gonna make me wooing you harder and more expensive," he said, laughing. There was still defeat in his voice.

"So that means we can still be friends?"

He nodded, fast and hard. "Of course. Besides, if Trill lives up to his reputation, you're going to need me for a friend."

A puzzled look swept across her face. "Why do you say that?"

"Because he's been known to drop a girl or two. You can Google the real newspapers to check. Until then, it's just a rumor because I'm not one hundred percent sure. But if that does happen and he drops you, I'm going to be the friend to catch you. Because that's what friends do. We help each other, and not because we'd look good in prom gear." He laughed again.

His words filled Patience's head, and she hoped there wasn't any truth to what he was saying about Trill.

"So . . . can I know the name of my possible knight in shining armor?"

"You can call me Z, short for Zion."

Now it was Patience's turn to be surprised, and jab back at him. "Zion? As in the multiple-award-winning choir boy who all the ladies love more than Cool J, Zion?"

"Du-du-da-dah," he sang like a superhero. "The one and only, or you can just call me the catcher. Get it catch-her?"

Patience was relieved now that she knew where she'd seen Zion before. He usually wore suits, complete with neckties and pocket squares, which is why she couldn't remember where she'd known him from, but he was one in the same as the guy she'd seen on TV many times performing gospel hits. She shook her head. He was as corny as his buttoned-up-too-high shirt, army haircut, and almost high-water jeans, but for the first time in a long time, she connected with someone with the same church roots as she had, and it felt good. The phone vibrated in her pocket again, and she pulled it out. Trill wanted to know where she was, and demanded that she check in at least once a day. If he cared so much, maybe, just maybe, Zion had been wrong about him. She hoped she was right.

19

SANTANA

Santana sat on Gulliver's sofa, thumbing through his CD collection. His taste was strange or "eclectic," as he'd called it. A singer she'd never heard before crooned through the speakers. She swore Gully had the soul of an old man, probably from being raised by his grandmother, which she believed was a good thing because he was a good person. They'd pulled off his plan for her to act sick, and she'd wound up with sympathy from her mother and Craig instead of another punishment. But now she had to do her part—learn about computers and databases.

"Here," Gully said, handing her a glass. "It's this drink called sorrel. They drink it a lot in the West Indies, and my grandmother swears by it."

Santana smiled at him. Ever since they'd met he'd introduced her to new things, and though she didn't care to admit it, he'd made her world larger.

"Thanks. So you ready to scream? You know I'm gonna drive you crazy. The only thing I know about computers is how to social network and e-mail."

He waved his hand at her and beckoned her to follow him. "You're smarter than you think, Santana. You just fight it."

She shrugged. He was right, but, again, it wasn't something she'd admit.

The house was quiet and dark and old. The scent of pine cleaner and bleach filled the air, bespeaking his grandmother's cleanliness. They passed an enclosed porch where she noticed pictures of Jesus, Martin Luther King Jr., and John F. Kennedy on the wall. That was enough to tell her that his granny was as old as her great-grandmother.

"In here," Gully directed, opening a door. "This is my bedroom—where all the magic happens, of course."

Santana entered the room laughing. Gulliver always made her smile, and never pushed up on her the wrong way. Then she wondered why. It wasn't that she was interested in him; it was that any other guy would've tried. They all did. For a second, a fraction of a minute, whether he found her attractive or not mattered.

"Why the look?" he asked, smiling.

She couldn't believe she'd slipped. She was only supposed to let the thought cross her mind, not register on her face.

"It's because of Pharaoh, right? Is it hard for you to be here when you know that he could pull up any second?"

She shook her head. She was fine with Pharaoh being outside and anywhere else. He was her boyfriend, and she had to trust him. That's what they'd established after he'd met her around the corner from her house and swore on his life that Nae had followed him to the cabins. But nothing happened, that's what he'd said, and she believed him. How could she not after comparing herself to Nae? Nae was hands down not the *it* girl.

"Good!" Gully said. "Have a seat." He pointed to a huge plush bed that looked as if it'd been decorated by Martha Stewart herself. In fact, as she took the room in, it resembled a magazine layout, and didn't look like it fit the rest of the house. Everything in it was high quality and state of the art.

"Oh, I forgot to tell you my grandmother's into home design and sewing. I know you can't tell from the rest of the house. That's because she's sentimental and wanted to keep everything just the way it was when my parents and grandfather were alive. You should see her room . . . if you think this one is something."

Commotion filtered in from outside. Gully walked over to the window and peered out. When he turned his face was frozen as if he was nervous or stuck.

"What's wrong? Who're the fools acting up now?" Santana changed her mind about sitting, and wanted to see what was going on. She turned toward the window.

Gully stood in front of her. "Santana, don't. Let's just get to work. It's very interesting."

"Un-uh. I just want to see."

He grabbed her wrist, then stared in her eyes. "No, you don't . . . and I don't want you to. You're worth too much, Santana."

She snatched away from him. Now she had to see what

was going on. In only three steps she'd made it to the window, cracked the blinds with two fingers, pressed her face to the opening, and discovered her world was a lie. To the left a violent dice game was in session. To the right was her man, and he was the biggest, nastiest liar she knew. He stood leaning against his car as usual with his legs slightly parted, and Nae was settled between them. They were kissing—full-fledged Frenching, like they were the only two in the world.

"Sorry," she said to Gully, then darted out of his room.

"No, Santana! Wait!" he called and ran after her.

"You no-good liar!" she spat like venom as soon as she opened the front door. She was moving so fast she didn't feel the steps underneath her feet, or the barren landscape. But she could feel her fist punching someone's face, that's how bad she wanted to. She hadn't even made it to him and Nae yet, but in her mind she'd already knocked them out. She tasted blood, revenge, and hate.

"Oh," Nae said, then slid behind Pharaoh and climbed through the open car window into the safety of the Charger.

"What up, shawty?" he asked, acting as if she hadn't seen anything, but unable to look at her.

"Santana, just come back inside. . . ." Gully stood to her right, reaching out for her.

Pharaoh stepped up, then walked toward Santana and Gully. She looked him up and down, then noticed something on the ground she could use to split his head. A huge rock. In one swoop, she picked it up.

"*Inside?*" Pharaoh asked Gully. "What, G, you pushing up on my girl or somethin?"

"Your girl?" Santana hissed, holding up the rock and aiming it at him. "Your girl's in your car . . . and I'm out of your life."

Pharaoh held up his hands in surrender. "Come on now, baby. You know it ain't like dat. I don't want her. She was just telling me a secret. Plus," he said, pulling out two tickets from his pocket, "I have VIP passes to Trill—yes, ya heard ya man, shawty, I said to Trill's surprise birthday party. Just for you!"

Santana mimicked the girls at her new school, and doubled over in laughter. Pharaoh must've thought she was still a fool. She'd seen him with her own eyes, and he knew she had, but he still was trying to play her? She shook her head, walked up on him and snatched the tickets from his hand. She pocketed them, walking back over to Gully.

"Gulliver, what's the word for someone trying to play you like you stupid when you not?"

"Patronize."

"Yeah, well, Pharaoh, don't try to patronize me or insult my intelligence."

Gulliver laughed. "Wow, Santana. I'm impressed. Seems you've already picked up a few words at your new school."

She nodded. "I only been there a couple days. I got the new vocab from you. I'm working on my lexicon."

Pharaoh put one hand in his pocket. He licked his lips and glared at Gulliver.

"Yo, G, shut up 'fore I slap you."

Santana aimed her rock. "Try it, and I'll bust your head."

Gulliver stepped in front of Santana. From the look on

his face and his body language it was obvious that he wasn't scared of Pharaoh. Not in the least.

"Look Pharaoh, we've known each other for a long time, buddy. And I know I may speak and dress differently from you, and that I view the world in a way that you don't, but I also know that we're from the same streets. You know me, just like I know you. And you know I'm many things, but I'm not a punk."

"And I ain't no punk neither, homeboy. I plays wit steel, partner. I'm from the skreets." Pharaoh bucked up.

Santana jumped in front of Gulliver, disgusted by Pharaoh's skreets, wits, and ain'ts. There was no way she was going to let him put his grimy hands on her friend. All of a sudden she saw him through a new lens. He was no longer sexy or cute or fine. His hood grammar was decidedly ignorant, and now she knew it. He just didn't do it for her anymore, and she knew he didn't deserve her. She held the rock high over her head, aiming it for his, then pulled it back, ready to bust him in the face. And in the blink of an eye, she threw it with all her might. Pharaoh jumped, blocking his face. Santana laughed. The rock landed in the street where she'd intended it to.

"You know what, Pharaoh? I'm not even mad at you. You're just dumb as hell-oh. But I am mad at me because you didn't deserve me and I wasted my time with you. I feel sorry for you. All you know how to do is hustle, and all hustlers end up in jail. Where I'm *not* headed." She looked at Gulliver. "Because of people like him and my stepdad. I'm not jail material. I'm Santana Jackson, and I'm too fly for that."

She laced her arm through Gully's and kept it moving.

20

DYNASTY

Rufus refused to be pushed in a wheelchair, and hobbled out of the hospital sicker than when he went in. His nose was stuffed from the cold he'd caught from the frigid air-conditioning, his stomach hurt because of the two-day hospital diet he'd been forced to endure, and he'd sworn he'd had an allergic reaction, an invisible rash that only he could see, because he'd been assigned a male nurse instead of the female one with the "nice butt." Dynasty walked next to him, holding his bag of goodies that she planned to chuck into the first garbage can she saw. She couldn't figure out why he was so hardheaded. He had a heart problem and high cholesterol, and had been warned that he was an inch from becoming diabetic. Still, he insisted on his usual snacks of chips, skins, and cupcakes. She shrugged. He wasn't going to get them. She didn't care how angry he'd be, and she'd never been afraid of him, so they were as good as gone.

"How we getting home?" asked Rufus, standing by the curb, looking into the parking lot.

Dynasty tossed his goodie bag into the trash. She held her hand over her eyes to shield them from the sun.

"There!" She pointed. "Here comes City now."

Rufus looked at her. "That's your boyfriend." It wasn't a question; he wasn't asking her. He was telling her.

She tilted her head and gave him a soft look. She didn't want to hurt him because she knew, deep down, he was crushing on her. But she didn't want to lie to him either. She'd spent both days in the hospital with him, and they'd developed quite a bond, especially after his family was a no-show and City had to pay someone to pretend they were Rufus's parent and sign the hospital release papers. She nodded. Yes, Rufus deserved the truth, and if he was really her friend he'd be happy for her.

"Kinda, but not really."

"Kinda, but not really? What's that? Either he is or he isn't."

"Well, no then. Since you put it like that."

"But you like him," Rufus said, waving his long arm in the air to get City's attention.

She nodded. "I do. He's been really good and sweet to me, plus—"

Rufus elbowed her. "He helped you get into a business, bought you a new dictionary and SAT book, and some clothes. That's all you talked about for two days. How can I forget?" He started walking to City's car, which was standing idle behind another that was picking up someone, too.

City jumped out of his car, and jogged to meet them.

"Dynasty! My man, Big Ruf. Nice to see you two," he said, taking Rufus's bag from Dynasty. "Dynasty, I'm so glad to see you. I can't wait to tell you about the new stock we have coming."

Dynasty smiled and gave City a half hug. She didn't want to rub their being together in Rufus's face. It was bad enough that she'd called City to see if he could pick them up.

"Oh, yeah. Here," he said, reaching into his back pocket. He handed Dynasty two tickets. "Look what I got! We're going to the party of the year! What I tell ya, baby? Your fam's got you covered."

Dynasty looked at the tickets and almost passed out. They were two exclusive passes to a personal surprise party for Trill—an invite-only event.

"How . . ."

"Trill?" Rufus said, finally reaching the front of City's car.

City pointed to the car. "My people . . . Meka."

People bounced through Dynasty's mind like a thorny Ping-Pong ball, tearing up her brain. "Your *people*?"

City nodded. "Yes, I told you I was bringing her to New York . . . to meet my other fam. Just like I introduced you to her because we're fam, me and you. We're almost related because of your aunt and my grandfather. Family. Isn't that right, Big Ruf?"

Rufus scratched his head, looking at Dynasty. He held open the back door of the car for her. "I don't know about all that, City. I'm her friend."

Dynasty reluctantly got into the car and made herself speak to Meka. She looked at Rufus through pained eyes, and was glad that she had him to lean on. He was her friend, he'd made that clear. City was her fam and business partner, and genuinely cared about her well-being and future, he just didn't genuinely like her the same as she did him.

"So you good with going to the party, Dynasty?" he called from the front, pulling off from the curb. "We got to make our money, fam. There's going to be a lot of people there who can help brand us and help take City Gear international."

Rufus grabbed her hand and squeezed it.

"You okay?" he mouthed.

She nodded. "City, I'm good with everything. You've made it all crystal clear."

21

PATIENCE

Meka whipped what Patience assumed was a borrowed car into Trill's driveway and began to drive the long stretch to the house. Music blasted throughout the luxury ride, sounding as crisp as the songs in the studio. Patience sat in her seat fighting a surfacing smile. She'd done the impossible again. She managed to sneak out of the house, and had plenty of time to spend with Trill. Bishop had been called out on an emergency, her mother was at a weekend women's auxiliary, and her sisters Faith and Hope had no choice but to back her *Mission Impossible* act once she'd called in a favor to Meka.

"So you gonna be cool, right?" Meka asked, pressing her G-stack Louboutins on the accelerator. Meka had re-hood-named the shoes because they were priced at almost one thousand dollars after taxes. "I'm only gonna be a few minutes away, with my girl Santana, if you need me."

Patience waved her hand. "I'm always cool with Trill. Besides, he told me to come anytime. Being his girl gives me an open-door policy."

Meka brought the car to a stop. "Oh, I know all about open-door policies, that's why I'm asking if you're gonna be cool. I've walked in many open doors to find the wrong person sitting on the other side. He does know you're coming, right?"

Patience opened the car door and slid out.

"He better after the way he keeps calling and texting and begging. I was just over here the other day and the day after I met—"

"Choir Boy. I know." Meka laughed. Patience had caught Meka up on her whole life story, including Zion and the girl from the studio. "Make sure you text or call me fifteen minutes before you're ready to leave, and I'll be here. By the way, thanks for the new bag. You didn't have to give me anything to come get you—or to check Faith and Hope, with they better-than-everybody selves. And Studio Girl better watch it too!"

Patience walked up the rest of the driveway to the house. Before she could make it to the steps, Countess showed her coal-black face.

"Oh . . . I . . . Trill didn't know you—I mean didn't tell me you were coming over," she stammered, clearly frazzled and nervous. "Come in, I'll go get Trill. He's . . . he's—oh, never mind, just follow me to my office, please. I'll alert him that you're here."

"Your office?" Patience didn't like the sound of Countess's voice or being treated like a business visitor. She'd been here plenty of times, and had been granted access to the house like she lived there. Now Countess was giving her the publicist demeanor? She pursed her lips and followed Countess through a door to the left of the foyer, a place Patience had overlooked the times she'd been there and had dismissed as a closet.

Papers were all over Countess's desk next to a coffee mug and computer, and a foot-high stack of files balanced on the corner it. Patience sat in the lone chair in front of the desk and wondered if she huffed and puffed could she make it fall down. A slight smile crept up on her then. The stack contained files of two kinds. Personal ones for her, Trill, T, and Teeny, which were all labeled in black capital letters, and business ones such as expenses, media, tours, and shows, which were marked in red lowercase letters. Then she noticed the one at the bottom of the pile, the one Trill must've had the most trouble with, the bright orange one, DAMAGE CONTROL. It was the only business file in caps.

"Oh . . . here," Countess said, handing Patience an envelope. "Those are from Teeny. They're tickets to Trill's surprise birthday party T and Teeny are throwing him. And because of your new status—future superstar—they're all plus-ones."

She smiled, but Patience could tell something was still wrong. Her cell phone buzzed, and Countess confirmed Patience's belief.

"One sec," she stammered again, leaving the room and closing the door behind her.

On the other side of the door, Patience could hear the low commotion of Countess's whispering orders and cursing in a hushed, angry tone. Footfalls, she assumed from Trill's flunkies and staff, sounded. All at once her stomach turned. Her gut was telling her something was very wrong. It was time she followed her instinct, she told herself, getting up from the chair and speed-walking through the door.

Amidst the rush of commotion, no one noticed her scour the house. Trill wasn't upstairs, downstairs, in the kitchen or backyard. She looked out the window at the pool house and thought she saw someone flash past at superhero speed. Patience knew that was where Trill was. No one had to verbally tell her; they were all speaking loud and clear once she bounded toward the back door.

"I asked you to wait in the office," Countess said, appearing from somewhere.

"What's good, lil momma?" Big Dude asked, trying to block the door.

Patience sidestepped them both, and flattened the grass under her rushed, heavy footsteps. She made it to the pool house in no time, and pushed her way inside. There was a lesson on the other side of the door. She had competition. A serious opponent who was trying to invade her space had fled but left reminders of herself behind. Sweet perfume still filled the air, a tube of very pale, almost white, glittery silver lip gloss was on the table, and a pair of shoes were under it. Without having to guess, Patience knew who her runaway barefoot contender was. The girl at the studio.

"Hey, lil momma! Come give me some love," Trill said, leaning against the wall in a pair of boxers, a wife-beater T-shirt, and house shoes.

Patience looked at him and only saw a red flash of pain. Countess ran into the room, then casually tried to slow her pace as if she hadn't just been hightailing it. Patience wished she could cut her in two with her eyes.

"Oh, I've been looking all over for my lip gloss. . . . I must've forgot it in here when I was taking a meeting," she lied, nervously retrieving the makeup from the table.

"When did you start wearing makeup?" Patience asked to rattle Countess and let her know that she knew she was lying. "Let me see you put it on. It looks like your color."

Countess looked at Trill, and he nodded. Reluctantly, she opened the cap and applied it. Against her coal-black skin, the almost-white silver gloss glittered on her lips looking like shimmering whiteout on black construction paper. Patience held up her cell phone and took a surprise picture of Countess.

"Beautiful," Patience lied. "Don't forget your shoes."

Countess's eyes stretched wider than Patience had ever seen. "Shoes? Oh. Oh. I must've forgot them too."

"You have to put them on for me. Have to!" Patience looked at the shoes under the table, clearly toddler small compared to Countess's super-sized feet.

"Ohhh," Countess gasped, following Patience's eyes to the ultra-high loud-pink heels. "I don't think I can wear those. . . . I mean, my feet are swollen. I don't think I can possibly get in those *now*."

Patience looked down at Countess's feet. She was already wearing high heels, and her feet were as slender as ever.

"You know what . . ." Patience looked at Trill, then at Countess. "You can't wear those because they aren't yours!"

She went to the table, snatched the shoes from under it, looked inside the shoe, and held them out to Countess. "You can't and never will be able to wear a six! You have to be an eleven at least."

She turned to Trill, and started walking toward him. Inches away from him, she ran her face alongside his and sniffed.

"Maybe they're yours?"

"Come on, lil momma . . ."

"You still smell like her." Patience threw the shoes at him and bounded out of the pool house. She ran the entire length of the driveway, calling Zion as she did.

"Patience. I was just thinking about you," he answered, happy to hear from her.

"Zion, can you pick me up . . . or have me picked up from Trill's? I really, really need a friend right now."

22

SANTANA

Santana rifled through her closet, under her bed, and everywhere else she could think of. The more she searched, the angrier she became. For the life of her, she couldn't find one of her boosting bags, and she badly needed to. She was officially done with Pharaoh, and was sure that everyone knew it by now, so she had a point to make. She needed to be the flyest girl in the party, and she couldn't wear anything she'd been seen in before. Her life had changed for the better, and she wanted to look like it. *Now* . . . She put her hands on her hips. *Where are my bags?* She had shopping to do—things she needed to "pick up." She knew it was risky after Meka had gotten caught, but what else could she do? She screamed at the top of her lungs, stomped her feet, and gave in to her hissy fit.

"What is it?" Craig bounded through her door. "Everything all right?"

Santana looked at him with spoiled-girl tears in her eyes. "My purses are gone! My Louis, Gucci, Chanel, Prada . . . gone. What am I going to . . ."

"I threw them away."

". . . do now? I have a party to go to." She hadn't heard Craig because she was too busy complaining.

He put his hands in his pocket, then raised his eyebrows. He exhaled. "I know you're not going to like this, but I threw them in the trash."

Now she jumped up and down because she didn't know what else to do.

"Why?"

Craig smiled. "Because you're my daughter now—stepdaughter—and I don't want you walking around here with fake bags. You don't need a purse if you can't carry the real thing. That's ridiculous, and the girls who do it look like it too. Like no one can tell that their purses are fake."

All she could do was stare at him. He had a point, but she didn't care. She didn't need her purses to impress anyone. She needed her bags so she could go boost her an outfit. And she needed one five minutes ago. Meka was due to pick her up any second.

"If you go look in the trunk of my car, you'll find new purses—real designer ones with certificates that you can register."

Now she was torn. Craig had just ruined her "shopping" plans, but had upgraded her bag collection. She couldn't be mad at him for wanting the best for her.

"So what am I going to do about shopping?"

He crinkled his brows. "What does shopping have to do with purses . . . ?" He held up his hand, then shook his head. "Don't tell me. . . . never mind. I don't even want to believe that you were out doing the same thing as your friend Meka." He pulled his billfold out of his wallet, and handed her a credit card.

"Look," he said, pointing in her face. "You better not tell your mom that I'm giving you this—she'd kill me." He bent forward and whispered in her ear, then stood up like he hadn't said anything. "Don't go a penny over, either. Not one cent."

Santana smiled. With the credit line he'd just given her, she could buy a fantastic outfit with designer shoes to match. She only hoped one of the bags he had in his trunk would match.

Meka had her game face on when she whipped the car into traffic. Santana could tell by her expression that she was in true booster's mode; she was a tad bit excited, a dash of nervous, and definitely a little scared of the possibility of being caught.

"Did you put your bag in the trunk? I didn't see you put it in the backseat."

Santana shook her head. "Craig threw them away because they were fake."

"What?" Meka almost crashed, then caught control of the car. "He did what?"

Santana reached into her pocket and pulled out the credit card. "But he gave me this to buy my outfit!"

Relief washed over Meka's face. "Girl, good. 'Cause I didn't feel like stealing anyway. After I got caught, I swore I was out of the game. And I would've been too, if I didn't think you needed me to help you get ready for this party. Plus, City's helping me out. I'm going to help him with putting some of his designs together. Me, him, and his fam Dynasty that he introduced us to, we're getting ready to do big things!"

Santana was happy for Meka. She'd finally met someone who really cared about her, had decided to stop boosting. There was only one thing left.

"So maybe you'll go back to school too?"

Meka looked at her like she was crazy. "Don't insult me like that. You know I'm a professional dropout. So where you want to head to first?"

"Phipps, but can you take me by Gulliver's first. There's something there I need to get."

She was nervous when she walked up on his porch and rang the bell. The unusually quiet street gave her too much time to wrestle with her thoughts, and she swore she could hear her heart beating.

"Santana! I didn't know you were coming by. What's up?" Gulliver asked, walking out on the porch wearing his usual college-boy gear.

"I'm going shopping. . . ."

He nodded. "Okay. What's new?"

"I'm going to pay for my things, not boost them," she remarked proudly.

A goofy smile lit up Gulliver's eyes. "Good for you. I'm proud of you. You're growing up."

She wilted her head and looked at her feet.

"So . . ." Gulliver asked. "You seem nervous."

Santana regained her fire. "Look Gulliver. I came over here to get something, and I'm not leaving without it."

His eyes bulged. "Okay. Tell me what it is, and I'm sure you can have it."

"A date. I want you to be my date for the party."

23

DYNASTY

Meretricious. Adjective. Mehr-ih-trish-uhs. Falsely attractive; gaudy. In a sentence: City's girlfriend's meretricious style and idea of grace would horrify any fashionista or refined person.

Dynasty smirked, sitting at her desk. She looked over at City, who was on the phone conducting a business transaction with some overseas garment manufacturers. They weren't ready for the big time yet, but were preparing for it.

"A smart person should map out their journey so they can be prepared," he'd said, and it'd made sense. She wondered now if that's what he'd done. Was that the reason he'd chosen her to help him, because he saw that she was young, naive, and hungry, and would follow him around like a lost dog? Loudly, she flipped through the dictionary, hoping the slightest sound would interrupt him. She didn't want his day to go smoothly. He'd disrupted her peace by revealing he was with Meka *after* he'd kissed her, and she couldn't think straight since.

Metaphor. Noun. Meht-uh-for. Figure of speech used in an imaginative way to compare two different things. She threw him a snarled look. *In a sentence: The* metaphor *"City's charm is an ocean of troubles that a young girl can drown in" suggests City's charm is misleading and dangerous, and too vast for a young girl to survive.*

He knocked on the desk to get her attention, then winked and gave her thumbs-up. It seemed that everything was going well—for him. *La-di-da and big deal,* she thought, diving back into her precious book.

The next word hit her with a vengeance, made the truth sink in deeper, and it hurt. It was her wrapped up in nine letters.

"*Malleable,*" she said aloud, trying to directly interrupt him. Flipping the pages hadn't bothered him at all, so she had to step up her game and her volume. "*Malleable. Adjective,*" she read in a loud, deliberately slow voice, careful to enunciate the word. "Mah-*lee-uh-buhl* or mal-*yuh-buhl. Capable of being shaped.*"

City looked over at her with a questioning look on his face. He shrugged his shoulders and held up his hands while he cradled the phone between his ear and shoulder.

What are you doing? he mouthed, then held his finger up to his mouth, shushing Dynasty.

She cranked up the decibel, and spoke at the top of her lungs. "*Malleable.* Used in a sentence: Dynasty was the most *malleable* of naïve girls; City discovered she could be formed into anything he wanted her to be—business partner and even a kissing cousin, whom he was not really related to." She slammed shut the dictionary, then threw it on the desk.

"Yo, Dynasty," he said, quickly hanging up the phone. "What's your problem? What's got your panties in a twist?"

Now she was upset. Not the type of angry that Rufus or Lipstick or Aunt Maybelline caused, but downright mad—as in the true definition of mad: insane.

"You." She stood and pointed at him, and wished the tip of her finger could shoot fire. "You have my panties in a twist. You played with my feelings, blew up my world until I thought I was flying high, then you shot me down. Made me fall face first—in love with you, then in the footsteps of Meka."

"What?" The expression on his face was incredulous, like he had no idea what she was talking about. "What I do? And you love me?"

She hadn't realized she'd just said the *L* word until it came from his mouth.

"All that time I thought you liked me. You said it. You showed it. You even asked me to go to New York, and I thought you wanted me to meet your mom. *And* you got us tickets for Trill's party."

"But I told you we were fam," said City as he walked over to her, then put his hands on her shoulders. "I told you Meka was my people . . . that I was going to introduce my *people* to my mom, and asked if you wanted to come, too, because you're fam. Fam means family, people means my girl. I guess you don't use that expression down here."

Dynasty looked deep into his eyes. "Then why did you kiss me?"

He turned his face to the side, and pretended to look out the window. Dynasty snatched away from him, and walked to the other side of the room.

"I didn't mean to mislead you, Dynasty. I didn't. I just saw so much of me in you so I wanted to help you because two years ago, when I was your age, no one helped me. I was wrong for kissing—"

"Kissing? Who was kissing? Us?" Meka burst in, sashayed over to City and pecked him on the cheek. She turned to Dynasty. "Or was it that guy you were with at the hospital?" She smiled. "I can tell he really likes you."

Dynasty held her breath for a second to compose herself. What she and City had was business, just business. So that's what it'd be from now on, she decided, pasting a *meretricious* smile on her face.

"No, Meka. Me and Rufus are friends—we're not dating or involved. Just real, one-hundred-percent friends. And kissing a friend would be as gross as kissing a relative. Wouldn't you agree, City?"

Meka shrugged. "Well, that's too bad. So who are you bringing to the party?"

"Party? You mean Trill's party?"

Meka nodded. City's face fell.

"Yes. Didn't you see that we gave you two tickets? One for you and one for a date. And I think I have just the outfit for you to wear. Wait until you see what me and City are wearing."

24

PATIENCE

Zion sat next to her in the family room on the plush suede sectional that was as deep as a mattress. Like two toddlers, their feet hung off of the cushions, unable to touch the floor. He'd come to her rescue without hesitation, and Patience was grateful, albeit ashamed. He'd warned her against Trill's womanizing ways, and she didn't want to believe him. A hollow slurping assaulted her eardrums, and she elbowed him. His extra-large milkshake—he'd assured her getting milkshakes would make her feel better—was gone, nothing but foam, and his mouth was still on the straw, pulling away on it as if more would magically appear.

"Are you feeling any better?" he asked Patience, while reaching for one of the many remote controls that lay between them on the sofa.

She looked at him. How could she answer no and yes at the same time and mean both? Yes, she was feeling a bit better knowing she wasn't a fool anymore and being able to decide if she wanted to be a part of Trill's trio— him, her and Damage. But she was also pretty down because she'd really liked Trill. She didn't want to rub it in Zion's face although he already knew.

"You know you can talk to me about anything, Patience. I'm here for you . . . and not because I'm happy that you called me to catch you."

"But he didn't drop me, so how can you catch me?" she asked, remembering his comment about his being there to catch her if Trill ever dropped her.

Zion scooted closer to her, but still stayed back a respectable distance. "That's the funny thing about it all. Proof that God works miracles. I prayed for a friend . . ."

Patience shot him a you've-got-to-be-kidding-me look.

"Okay. I prayed for a girlfriend like you. Someone who was strong, in the church, and someone who'd be smart enough to jump out of a bad situation and not wait to be dropped from one."

"You just think we'll look good in matching prom gear—your words, remember?"

Zion began to laugh, then held up his hand, signaling Patience to wait for a moment. He pointed to the TV and pressed the volume on the remote.

"Look . . ."

Patience bounced up and down in her seat. "Your new video. Wow! Isn't it time for hip-hop now? You've crossed over, Zion. Crossed over to mainstream without compromising your values." She liked that. She loved that he was rooted and secure in his religious values and beliefs. She admired him for sticking to the music he wanted to sing, though she enjoyed singing secular. "I'm proud of you."

Zion reached over and grabbed her hand. She squeezed his.

"Hey! What are you two doing watching that worldly mess in my house? Don't you understand whose home you're in, young man? I thought you'd be a better example for my daughter!" Bishop boomed in his deep, condescending voice from the archway.

Zion jumped.

Patience hung her head.

Bishop laughed.

"I'm just kidding," he teased, shocking Patience. She'd never heard her father joke about worldly music or his daughters having male company over without being chaperoned. In fact, she couldn't think of him ever joking about anything. "I know you're one of the good guys. Glad to have you over, Zion." He turned his head toward the television, then walked over and sat on the edge of the sectional. "That's your new song. Good work. Good work, son. We need more youth like you in the church."

Patience watched in awe as Bishop and Zion exchanged small talk. She was sure the man in front of her wasn't her father, he couldn't have been. He'd kicked off his shoes, sat back and crossed his legs, and began nodding his head to a few rap videos.

"Who are you?" she finally asked her dad, making sure to mask her question as a joke. "Bishop doesn't allow us to listen to this type of music," she explained to Zion.

"But that doesn't mean I don't listen to it," he admitted, shocking her again. He looked at Patience and smiled. "How do you think I keep up with what's going on in the world? You ever wonder how I incorporate rap lyrics and rappers' and singers' names into my sermons? Well, I keep up. Must stay young if I want to reach the young. Isn't that right, son?"

Zion nodded; then his eyes stretched.

Trill was on the television talking about his upcoming album, and Patience was about to run for her life. She closed her eyes, then covered her ears, but she couldn't block the truth. Right there, in front of Bishop, was a picture of Patience and Trill splashed across the screen—the same picture that had been circulating since the award show.

A reporter spoke. "It seems that this unknown girl won't be unknown for long. She was once suspected of being Trill's girlfriend, but now sources have confirmed that they recorded a song together. Here's a sample Trill's record company was nice enough to let us air."

Bishop stopped breathing. Patience held her breath. Zion jumped up, shouting, "Yes, Lord! You gave her a voice, and she's using it the way You see fit."

Patience didn't know what to do. She was scared. But in seconds her mood switched. It changed as soon as a new picture was splashed across the screen. One of Trill and Damage, his reported real girlfriend. They were spotted together kissing in the airport last night. It seems they'd snuck away for an overnight getaway.

"I'm hurt, Patience," Bishop admitted. "I'm hurt and ashamed. How can I lead a church if I can't lead my family?"

Zion interrupted. "Did you hear the lyrics, Bishop? Did you really listen? Patience was ministering, asking God to save us and not let the streets be our master."

Bishop's eyes went from Zion to Patience. "Is that true, Patience?"

She nodded.

Bishop laughed and clapped, jumped up and down, and became human in front of her eyes. Finally he stopped, held out his arms and spread them wide.

"Yes! Yes! I always prayed that you'd sing again. I may not like the rap stuff on that song, but anyone who's ministering on whatever kind of song has my approval and backing." He beckoned her with his hands. "Come give Daddy a hug."

He'd never called himself that, and it moved Patience. Scooting off the sofa, she made her way to Bishop and got lost in his huge arms like she did when she was a little girl. In the warmth of his embrace, she felt confident and daring.

"So does that mean I can go to the party—Trill's party—with Zion? They're going to play that song there, and I need to be there to show my support . . . and maybe minister to one or two of them. Trill's soon-to-be sister-in-law used to go to our church, and she's asked me to work on a few songs with her."

"No," Zion answered for Bishop. "You can't go to the party with me . . . not unless you promise to accompany me to the January award show I've been practicing for— maybe accompany me on stage, and we can do a full Christian remake to you and Trill's rap song. And you have to be my prom date."

Bishop held Patience back at arm's length. "I think this young man's on to something. And I'm almost sure he's talking about the Stellar Awards. You've been on the Black Star Power red carpet, now you need to even that out for the Lord."

25

SANTANA

The red carpet felt good under her five-inch stilettos. She smiled bright, snuggled next to Gulliver, as cameras flashed and limousines pulled up with various celebrities and other important people exiting from them. They were called stars as they made their way into the high-security country club that Trill's brother had rented for the evening. And that's exactly what she felt like: someone important who walked alongside a person worthy of her.

Gulliver fidgeted with his clothes, making sure his shirt was straight and his pants were just so.

"Why did you bring me again?" he asked Santana for the fifth time that night.

"Because you're important to me, Gulliver. And I didn't think anyone else would look good with this dress," she teased, swirling in her backless beaded gown that was exceptionally light despite all the beadwork.

"And because you think I match this, too," he asked, running his fingers through her short hair.

She'd ditched her weave, her makeup, and her hoodness for the evening, and even she had to admit she felt better being natural. Studying had also improved her self-image. She'd noticed it the first time she'd been able to have a conversation without ain'ts and the sassiness—ghettoness—she was known for around the way.

"This way." Gulliver ushered her through the crowd, and found them a seat.

He looked good. Really cute. When she'd gone shopping, she picked him up an outfit, too. A nice soft-blue brushed linen that looked suede. It was top of the line like his attitude and intelligence. She'd kept in mind how smart he was when she decided to dress him, and knew she had to match the clothes with the guy.

"So this is a date? A real date?"

A waiter stopped at their table, filled their goblets with water, and told them dinner would be served as soon as the guest of honor arrived and a speech was given.

"Do you want it to be a *date* date? Don't you think I need to complete Gulliver's Finishing School first?" she teased and flirted at the same time, puckering her lips a little more than necessary when enunciating her words. "Aren't you too advanced for me, college boy?"

His expression was charming when he looked at her. "You've schooled me, too. Kinda taught me what I want in a girl."

Now it was Santana's turn to correct him. "Kinda?"

Gulliver laughed.

Santana spotted Meka walking on the other side of the

room. "One sec, okay? I see Meka and her boyfriend over there, and I don't want to be ghetto and yell across the room." She stood. "*But* if you need to know now whether this is a date or not, I don't mind if you don't."

She couldn't find Meka anywhere. Santana was sure she was navigating through the crowd the correct way but, somehow, Meka and City had disappeared. She snapped her fingers. If she and her BFF were anything alike, she knew she was touching up her makeup in the ladies' room. She looked around the party for signs of a restroom. A dull green glow caught her eye a few feet to her left, and she worked her way through the partygoers to reach it. Before she could turn down the corridor, someone grabbed her. Instinct told her to swing. His voice stopped her.

"Are you my birthday surprise, lil momma?" Trill asked.

Santana almost jumped out of her skin. He was her all-time favorite, and much cuter in person than she could've imagined.

He grabbed her hand, pulled her down the corridor, and out of a hidden exit. "Come with me. Don't worry, you're in good hands."

Like a fool, she followed him. She didn't know where she was going, and didn't care. Being in the presence of such celebrity and fineness, she couldn't help herself, nor did she want to.

"This way," he advised. "Duck, lil momma."

She ducked down into the limousine, careful not to hit her head on her way in—that would've been too embarrassing for her to handle.

"So . . ." she clasped her hands, trying to be as ladylike as she could to hold back the groupie in her. "Happy Birthday!"

Trill smiled. "Thanks. What's your name, lil momma?"

"Santana."

He nodded. "I like that. Like Carlos Santana? One of the best musicians on the planet?"

She nodded. "Yes, like him."

"So can I call you sometime?" Trill asked, looking at his watch. "I hate to be late for my own party, but I had to talk to you. Had to."

Santana smiled. Sure, he could call her. Anytime. Then her mind switched back to Gulliver, the good guy who she was definitely falling for and had been nice enough to accompany her to the party, and feed her brain and confidence. But she couldn't resist Trill.

"Take my number," she told him, wondering if she'd ever get over her attraction to bad boys with swagger. She wasn't yet accustomed to her new life. Yes, she liked her school, was falling for Gulliver, and was even considering keeping her natural look. But she had to question what she really wanted now. Who the real Santana was— the Santana minus boosting, the hood, and Pharaoh. As she sat there getting ready to exchange numbers with Trill, she changed her mind. She wasn't Santana from the block anymore who could blame bad choices on others or her surroundings. She was Santana who'd learned to love herself and know her worth. She was above a groupie, had higher standards than gold-diggers and half-dressed hoochies—and she was no longer those girls. She was a mature responsible teen; one who knew whom and what she wanted: Gulliver, and to educate and better herself. "You know what, I think I'll pass. Sorry."

She made her way back into the party to Gully, the cute college boy who was helping to change her life, her opinion and what she found attractive in a guy. She'd had it all together, and if she ever had a doubt in her mind while talking to Trill, Gulliver erased it when he stepped up and greeted her with a kiss.

26

DYNASTY

"Rufus!" yelled Dynasty. "You're going to make us late."

Rufus rolled out of the cab, taking his sweet time. He wasn't enthused about going to the party, and had told Dynasty so. He was only going because she needed him to. Because he was her friend.

"I'm coming. My feet hurt, and I don't like wearing these stupid pants."

Dynasty shot him machetes with her eyes. He'd complained all day and night, but had been super excited when she'd asked him to go and offered to buy him pants—which cost her two thumbs because he could only shop in a big man's store—and shoes—which set her back at least a couple of weeks pay because he wore a size sixteen and a half. "I thought we agreed not to use that word anymore. It's a bad word, Rufus. Bad." She grabbed his sleeve and pulled him toward the party.

"Only if it can hurt somebody's feelings," he said. "Stupid can't hurt pants."

She walked with purpose at top speed, ignoring his statement. After he'd admitted to feeling stupid, they'd chucked the insult to the bad-word list and promised never to use it again. He hated it as much as she despised being called poor and burnt-black. She stopped in front of where the party was being held, and straightened Rufus's navy tie. Then she coached him.

"Be yourself, Rufus. You're—*we're*—just as good as anyone here. Don't fidget or complain, and don't forget to start using your new words. That's the only way to learn them and make them a part of your vocabulary." She rose on her tiptoes and pulled him down toward her at the same time. That was the only way she could reach his cheek because he was so tall. She kissed him on the cheek.

"Thanks for coming with me, Rufus. Thanks more for being my friend."

They made their way to the red carpet, posed for their pictures, and soaked in their surroundings. Neither one of them had ever been to a celebrity function or in a place where they had to dress up. Not like this. Dynasty adjusted her white strapless gown, dusted her matching kitten heels, and clutched her purse tight under her arm. In Rufus's words, she was beautiful, and she felt like it. The dress clung to her like second skin, accentuating her almost negative curves, and made her appreciate being so thin. There was no way she could've pulled the outfit off if she were three pounds heavier.

Rufus pointed as soon as they entered the luxurious

room where the party was being held. "There's City. You sure you gonna . . . I mean are you sure that you're *going* to be okay? I mean . . . he's with that girl."

She followed Rufus's index finger, and saw City and Meka circulating. The sight of them together didn't bother her as much as she'd thought. She pasted a faux grin on her face.

"Smile, Rufus. Act like we're having a ball," she instructed when City looked her way. She waved back and almost bit her lip when she saw that he and Meka were headed to her and Rufus.

"Dynasty!" Meka greeted before they were close. "You look so nice. That dress is hot on you."

Though she couldn't stand the fact that City was with Meka when she'd thought he was going to be with her, it was hard to dislike Meka. She was nice, genuine.

"Thanks, Meka. You look nice, too. I'm so excited to be here," she admitted.

Meka paused. "Dynasty? Can I ask you a favor? My friend is here. . . . You remember Santana? Well, she goes to Winchester Hills Preparatory School now, and she needs some help with English—comprehension, spelling." She shrugged. "You know, words. You think you can help her?"

Rufus elbowed Dynasty. "Ain't that the school you wanna go to so bad?"

Dynasty gave him a look.

"Sorry. Isn't that the school you've been trying to get into?"

"Oh. That'll be no problem. Craig, her stepdad, has the major hookup and political connections. If you help her, I'm sure he'll work out something. He sprung me from jail, won my case, and never put up a dime or stepped in the courtroom. He's a legal heavyweight with straight stacks of money."

City butted in. "Dynasty, step over here and let me talk to you about some business." He excused them, then took her hand, and led her to a dark corridor off the main room. "Listen, about your question . . ."

"I'm listening, City." She leaned against the wall, preparing to hear the worst, and braced herself for it.

"It's been bothering me for a minute. But I feel that it's only right that I tell you. I kissed you because I liked you." His admission was sweet, honest, and heartfelt. She could see it in his eyes.

"Liked?"

He nodded, then shook his head no. He was clearly confused, and seemed nervous. Something she'd never seen before. Anxiousness wasn't supposed to look good on guys with status and swagger, but for some reason, it made City more appealing. He hit his fist against the wall in defeat. "No. I like you. A lot. That's why I tried to make and keep you as my fam. I figured if I didn't act on it . . . then . . . you know, there's Meka, and I was with her first, and that wouldn't have been fair to you or her."

Her confidence rose. "Spit it out, City. Then, what?"

"If I made you my fam I could always keep you around—we could never break up."

Dynasty took him in with her eyes. He was just as beautiful as when she'd first seen him, and she knew that she had to step up her game.

"Look, City. I was once told there are two types of

people in the world. People who make things happen and people who watch things happen." She stepped up to him. "I stopped being a spectator days after I met you, thanks to you."

City laughed. "You got me, but what I said was there are two ways to live. You either make it happen, or watch it happen."

"Well, watch me make it happen then." She leaned forward, wrapped her arms around City, and kissed him on the cheek. He was right; if they made each other family they would never break up. And for the life they were building—the business, the cash she made while working with him and could save for her future—she couldn't afford to lose. Quickly she let him go, then looked back the way they'd come. "We got something good, City. And as you said, you have Meka . . . and I have Rufus. He may not be you, but he's my friend, and I don't want to hurt him. While we both know he doesn't have your swag, he certainly has a heart like yours. Both of you are good for me. Now let's go out here and party, and celebrate our futures."

She walked away, happy with her decision. She didn't know what she was going to do about Rufus's crush. Hadn't a clue on how to handle knowing that City liked her. All she knew was that life was a game, and education and friends were the jackpots. And she was going to win.

27

PATIENCE

Fans screamed and cheered when Patience and Zion exited the limousine, and reporters thrust their microphones in their faces. Zion stepped back, allowing Patience the limelight. The paparazzi wanted her. Somehow, her and Trill's song had already leaked completely, and the gossip channels had made her name swim through the hip-hop who's-who channels.

Patience smiled, not sure of what to do. But she did remember Bishop's advice. *Keep your head up. Remember who you are. And always be kind to God and His people. It's because of Him that you are who you are, and it will be up to the people whether you stay or not. Life deals hard blows—always soften your fans' and followers' blows with a smile.* She looked to Zion for assistance, but received more than she was hoping for.

"So are you two an item?"

"Zion, aren't you performing at the Stellar Awards? Rumor has it that you're up for a few different awards this year."

"Patience? How does the daughter of a famous bishop get into hip-hop music?"

"Zion, is it true that you and Trill got into an altercation over Patience?"

They finally escaped to the safety of the building. His hand was on her back, her cheek was resting on his shoulder, and both of their stomachs hurt from laughing so hard. She couldn't believe paparazzi were so nosy, literally making things up as they went along.

"Lil Sis!" T, Trill's brother, greeted her and Zion. "What's this I hear about you replacing our family with this fool?" He mean-faced Zion, looking him up and down as if he were garbage.

"Fool? Who you calling a fool, corner boy?"

Patience's heart fell to her knees. She didn't know how to handle a situation like this, and felt responsible.

"Don't do that, y'all," Teeny said, appearing from behind T, then giving Patience a hug.

Zion and T laughed, then gave each other a brotherly hug, pounding each other on the back the way that men do.

"Sorry," T said. "I couldn't help it. You might as well get used to it 'cause people make up stuff all the time. I already heard the rumor about Z and my brother fighting over you."

Zion nodded. "They even spread rumors in the Christian genre. You ready for this?"

Patience wasn't sure. And if she hadn't questioned herself and preparedness before, she was certainly getting ready to. Trill was strolling their way with Damage by his side. The tension was thick enough to fill the room when the couples—Patience and Zion, and Trill and Damage—spotted each other, and doubled in depth when they were eye to eye.

"S'up?" asked Trill.

Zion's feet were shoulder width apart, and his stance was strong. Patience couldn't believe how defensive he could be. Or was he just being protective and territorial?

"What's up?" replied Zion.

"Nothing," Damage had the nerve to say.

Patience touched her short sleeve kimono, then fingered the chopsticks holding her bun in place. Her eyes brightened.

"Everything's up!" She put her arm through Zion's, then veered off, but not before looking over her shoulder at Teeny. "Call me, Sis, when you're ready to write those songs. And my dad says he'll see you guys at church on Sunday."

T popped Trill upside his head. "You a fool, homeboy. You could've had her. She's a real lady." He nodded toward Patience. "Sorry, Sis."

Teeny waved too. "See y'all at the head table!"

Patience looked at Zion. She'd managed to talk him into getting his hair cut. She'd convinced him to wear a pair of funky jeans, a high-end silk couture T-shirt, and a fresh pair of loafers that cost more than he'd ever spent on shoes, but there was one thing she was glad she couldn't change. Who he was inside.

"You know if you keep this up, you may just have a date for the prom after all."

Zion winked. "And you may just have a real boyfriend that you can take home."

BOYFRIEND SEASON

Kelli London

ABOUT THIS GUIDE

The following questions are intended to
enhance your group's reading of
BOYFRIEND SEASON.

Discussion Questions

1. Santana, Dynasty, and Patience all took boys to the party that their friends or family wouldn't have approved of. Do you think their choices were courageous or not?

2. If someone tried to persuade you to date someone who'd make you look good, but not make you feel better about yourself, what would you do? Would you be brave enough to say no even if it meant losing your friends and popularity?

3. From outside appearances Santana was the "it" girl; she had looks, clothes, and was very popular. But did she really feel like the "it" girl, or do you think her self-esteem and self-direction were low?

4. Santana had a bad illegal habit that afforded her the ability to fit in and wear expensive designer clothes. How important do you think it is to fit in? Or is it better to be yourself and let others judge you based on your character not your material possessions.

5. Dynasty, though very smart, lived in conditions other than ideal. Do you think her studying the dictionary, planning years ahead for college, and making sure she stayed on the right path was a

good plan for a girl her age? How much thought
have you given to your future?

6. Dynasty's parents weren't in the picture. Do you
think that attributed to her being a little angry,
and oftentimes mean toward Rufus?

7. Sometimes friends have the best intentions, but
awful judgment. Do you think Silky had Patience's
best interest and family dynamics in mind when
she introduced her to Trill? Why?

8. Patience's dad was very overprotective. Do you
think he just wanted the best for his daughter, or
did he just want to stomp on her fun and indepen-
dence?

9. If a person's friends reflect who a person is deep
down, should Patience have judged Trill for the
"smoking, drinking, and rowdy" company he
kept?

10. *Boyfriend Season* addressed a lot of issues, including popularity, religious beliefs, growing up in
households with different family dynamics (single
mother, married parents, and no parents), friends
who indulge in illegal activities, peer pressure,
wrong vs. right, etc. How do you feel about all the
issues? If you were Santana, Patience, or Dynasty
would you have done anything differently? Did
they do the right things?

Don't miss Kelli London's newest novel,

Uptown Dreams.

Coming in December 2011.

Applications have been sent. Interviews have been given. Tryouts are just about over. And La-La, Reese, Ziggy, and Jamaica are ready for Harlem Academy of Creative and Performing Arts, where dreams aren't meant to be dreamt, they're dreamt to be realized. But now that their passions have become work and the competition is thick and steady, do they have what it takes to stay and realize their dreams?

Turn the page for an excerpt from *Uptown Dreams* . . .

LA-LA NOLAN

"I don't sing, I sang."

"Lexus and Mercedes, get off my feet before you get murked!" I warned my two sisters, shaking my legs one at a time, trying to break loose from their three- and four-year-old grips. It was too early for a foot ride, and I needed to get out the door and make tracks to get to school.

"Please, La-La," they sang in unison. "Foot ride. Foot ride. Foot ride!" they chanted.

"I. Said. Get. Off." I shuffled my feet one at a time, enunciating each word while alternately swinging my legs back and forth. Reaching down, I pressed my hand against Mercedes's forehead and pushed it with all my might.

"Boom-Kesha," she yelled out to our mother. "La-La murked me!"

Her snitching really set my fire, so I swished my legs one at a time as if I were punting a football. Lexus was my first successful attempt. With a harder kick and powerful shake and swoop, I managed to break her grasp, then watched in semi terror as she slid across the linoleum and connected with the painted concrete wall. The top of her head met the dent-proof wall first, colliding with a thump that I was sure she'd cry from.

"Whee!" she shouted, surprising me, then jumped up and came back for another turn.

"Me too. Me too," Mercedes pleaded. "Slide me, too."

I pointed at Lexus like that Celie chick from that old *Color Purple* movie when she gave that ancient Mister dude that Hoodoo sign. Lexus froze in her tracks. Four out of six of my siblings were terrified of that hand gesture because they believed everything they saw on TV, and they were sure it was magic of some sorts. Well, I'd made them believe I had that power because it worked to my benefit whenever they rode my nerves.

"*Whatever you done to me,*" I threatened, parroting Celie's line from the movie, making my voice deep, and stretching my eyes wide.

Lexus ran out screaming like she was on fire. Then Mercedes started to cry, setting free her slob and nose mucus dams.

"*Ill,*" I said. Her nose and sides of her mouth were running with clear and yellow gook. "Now you better get up. I don't want your cooties on my clothes."

She unwound herself from my leg, got off my foot, and whooshed away like a fire truck, screaming down the hall sounding like a siren. "Cootiescootiescooties!"

"Henrietta!" my mother's voice carried into the room. "Henrietta?"

Lexus came back to the door, peeking her head in. Then Alize, Remi, and Queen showed up, followed by King, crawling his way through their legs. I shook my head. My siblings were beautiful and smart, though many would never know it because my mother had cursed them. She had named them after liquor and luxury cars, or had given them aristocratic titles like we hailed from a monarchy instead of a New York housing project. But, the truth of the matter was, she'd done what so many others do: named her children after things she'd wanted but would never have.

"Henrietta! Heifer, I know you hear me," Boom-Kesha's—I mean, Momma's—raspy Newport voice floated into the room.

"You better answer her, La-La," Remi warned. She was thirteen, ten months younger than me, but so much older than anyone in the apartment. She'd been sick for months, diagnosed with cancer, and it was hellish, making her grow up faster than she should've. I would've done anything to take it away from her. Remi tightened up the headscarf she wore to hide her head after her hair began to fall out in big clean patches. "Her panties have been in a twist ever since she woke up, something about the city cutting her benefits. Like we was gonna be able to get welfare forever." She crossed her arms and sucked her teeth.

"You okay?" I asked, ignoring my mother calling me. I didn't like the coloring of Remi's skin. It was starting to gray like my grandfather's before he died.

Remi nodded. "I'm good. I just wish I had hair like yours. It seems too strong to fall out."

"Henrietta!" Boom-Kesha boomed again.

I touched my head, wishing I could give my hair to Remi. "Well, I wish I had your teeth. They're so pretty and white—so straight."

"Henrietta!"

"Henrietta? Don't shu 'ear you mami talking to ju?" Paco, my mother's bootleg, pretending-to-be-Spanish boyfriend poked his head into the bedroom, and asked in his borrowed Spanglish. The man was crazy. Just because his skin was light and sun-kissed, his hair was straight, black and silky, and people mistook him for Dominican, he'd reinvented himself as one. He even walked around with a Dominican Flag wrapped around his head at the Puerto Rican Day parade, complaining that New York didn't give the Dominicans a holiday. But, I guess—for him—it was cool. If he could pretend to be a real full-grown man and get away with it, he could lie about being anything else.

I looked at Paco, pointing to my ears. "Que?" I asked him *What?* in Spanish, pretending to buy into his fabricated heritage.

"Oh. Ju ears stopped up this morning? Up giving singing lessons all night to get free tutoring, chica? No problemo. I splain to ju mami for ju."

I pasted a fake smile on my face and smirked a thank-you. Everybody in the house had bought my lie. I had them all thinking that I was receiving tutoring so I could keep up in the fancy performing-arts school I'd been offered a full scholarship to after the director heard me singing on the train. The Harlem Academy of Creative and Performing Arts, aka CAPA, was a school that was supposed to make me and my mother Boom-Kesha's dreams come true; it was going to help make me a star and help her milk some money from some bourgeois art society that dished out funds to kids like me—teenagers who showed talent and promise, and didn't mind extra training to get into highfalutin Julliard—the it college that had recently showed interest in my voice. My mother was undoubtedly going to smoke and drink up the "extra" money, or use it on whatever her real addiction was. All I wanted was to get my teeth fixed, which was the reason I'd told them the tutoring lie. Really, I'd been hanging out in the adult singing spots in Greenwich Village, scouting singers I could one day sing backup for and, hopefully, stack my money for an orthodontist.

"Good lookin', Paco," I said, grabbing my book bag, and heading to the door.

"Henrietta!" My mom's voice stopped me before I could put my hand on the knob.

"La-La, La-La, La-La!" I sang to her. I don't know why I had to remind her of the name she crowned me with. She was the one who said I sang like a bird and dubbed me La-La, as if I could've afforded one more reason for the kids to tease me. It was bad enough my teeth were raggedy, and I was so skinny the thick girls started calling me Anna—short for anorexic. I'd been jonesed about my lack of weight forever, but not my grill because I kept my mouth closed as much as possible.

"Make sure you bring a weapon with you, and don't take the elevator because the gangs have it sewed up. I don't want you to be a victim—you're my star."

No, I'm your paycheck. Your ticket out of the projects.

"Me, Paco, Alize, Remi, Lexus, Mercedes, Queen, and King will be waiting outside when you get home. 'Cause if that wench, Nakeeda, from last year wants it, we'll give it to her. I ain't above dusting a kid, and her raggedy mother too."

"Word, La-La," Remi added from behind my mother. "I may be sick, but I can get it in. I won't even have to put my hair in a ponytail 'cause ain't enough left to pull out," she teased, but I felt her pain.

I mouthed *I love you* to Remi, then feigned a smile and looked at my mother. Her intentions were good, but that's all they'd ever be—intentions. She really didn't have a desire to better herself or get us out of the projects. We were living the project stereotype. I felt sorry for her and us, her children. It was sad that everyone, including my family, had started calling her Boom-Kesha, because every time someone looked up—boom! Kesha was pregnant by a different man, then gave the child a ghetto first name and a different daddy's surname, except for me. I was named after my grandmother. What was worse was that my mother preferred the moniker.

"I'm good. Cyd will be with me."

Cyd was my girl, my sister from a different mother. We were beyond best friends, and we rocked out—boys, parties, dreams, it didn't matter. And together, we were going to rock Harlem Academy, show 'em what we were made of, just like I planned to show Ziggy, the cute dude I'd met in the admissions office, what I was made of.

REESE ALLEN

"I'm a musician second, and a producer first."

5 A.M. *Five ay-em. Five o'clock in the morning! Is she serious?* I peeled open my eyelids, and looked at the beaming red numbers, then closed them again. It was way too early for anything, especially getting up.

"C'mon, Reese!"

Clap. Clap.

"It's time to practice!"

Clap. Clap.

Oh my god. Oh my god. She was serious and in Mrs. Allen form like *whoa*. What was up with her waking me before sunrise and Sandman the wino's bedtime? I would've done anything to go back in time if high school was going to mean this.

Clap. Clap. Clap.

"Perfect practice makes perfect. Up-up-up!"

Oh, no. Not the triple claps. I knew what that meant. First slapping her hands together as loudly as possible, and now her hand was on my shoulder, shimmying me from side to side as if shaking me was gonna make me want to get up. I crossed my eyes, and cursed in my head. Was she certifiably crazy or just really enthused? I'd *just* gone to bed at midnight. Had just hit the pillow five stinking hours ago because she'd insisted that I practice cello, piano, violin, and the sax until *she* was satisfied. But I wasn't surprised. It was always about her. My life was hers.

I don't know how I got past her and her incessant clapping, but, somehow, I managed to whir by her in a flash, but not before noticing she had a name tag pinned to her lapel. MRS. ALLEN, DIRECTOR. There was no way I was going to pull up to Harlem Academy with her. It was bad enough I had to attend the school she directed instead of the one I wanted to go to—Bronx Science, which was hard to get into, and you needed to be borderline genius to be a student there. I also didn't need anyone to know I was her daughter.

Before the shower's spray rained on the bathtub floor, I'd worked a shower cap around my bobby-pinned wrapped hair, sloshed a facial mask on my face, and stuck waterproof headphones in my ears. I'd played classical music last night; my mother's favorite. This morning, my choice; the tracks I'd been sneaking and working on behind her back—hip-hop and hardcore rap. The beats bumped in my ears loud enough to rattle my eardrums and allow the bass to vibrate my skeletal system. If Mommy Dearest could hear it, and knew I'd produced them with Blaze, my boyfriend she also knew nothing about, she'd topple to the floor like a house of Cheerios boxes in a windstorm.

"Reese, you've been in there almost an hour!" The boom of her fists shook the bathroom door, and I knew it was time to make an appearance.

With bobby pins removed, my hair flowed down to my elbows, cascading across my shoulders and hiding the small earbuds I'd stuck deep in the canals of my ears. I pulled out the piano bench, lifted the lid covering the ivory keys, sat down, and turned up my iPod all at once. Then I played. I straight grooved and allowed the piano to drown out the thump-thump-thump of the hip-hop that caressed my soul. Jay-Z, Drake, T.I., and Kanye all accompanied me as I stepped into the music like a pair of comfortable slippers. Beethoven had never flowed from my fingertips like this. I'd remixed his classical concerto with the hip-hop greats, and it was funky. Mozart was next, with a dash of Bach added for flavor and a touch of Pharrell for color.

"What's that, Reese? I've never heard the greats like that before." Her hands were on her hips, and her smart shoes were tapping.

Yeah. This is hip-hop, baby. I cut my eyes at her. To my surprise, she was enjoying the flow. But only because she didn't know I'd mixed classical and hip-hop. If she'd known that, she would've had a straight fall-to-her-knees and wiggle-on-the-floor conniption fit. Immediately, I stopped playing, closed the lid on the ivories, and got up.

"That's a piece I'm working on for Julliard," I lied, and then snatched up my knapsack. "I'll meet you at the school." *After I cop a new mixer to produce these new beats, I added in my head.* I had a competition coming up, and I planned to win.

She wanted Julliard.

I wanted hip-hop.

May the best woman win.

ZIGGY PHILLIP

"I dance like no one's watching so everyone will."

Beep. *Beep.*
The cars blew by and their tires spit water from the pavement. On my left, I could see the street-cleaning truck barely moving as it washed the streets.

Beep. Beep.

"Hurry up, yo! Don't make me have to get out this car," some disgruntled driver was yelling at the car in front of him.

Looking at the fight I was sure was about to jump off, I stepped into the street without looking. Someone laid on their horn, then shouted at me. *Dumb move.*

"Yo. Yo. You better watch where you going!" A cabbie's head was out the window, yelling at me in the middle of traffic on one-two-five, One-hundred-twenty-fifth Street—Harlem, New York.

I banged on the hood of the yellow cab, a sight rarely seen up here.

"Yo, back at you! Who you talking to like that? Man, this is a hundred-and-twenty-fifth street—Harlem—my playground. You better watch where you're going or take your butt back downtown where it's safe."

I crossed in front of the car, and waited in the middle of the street for the other morning traffic to pass. Who crossed at the corner anyway? Not me or the dozens of other people straddling the yellow lines dividing one flow of vehicles from the other. This was uptown, baby, where we did what we did our way.

"Youngin'!" Sandman, the official unofficial mayor of Harlem, called from a milk crate he'd climbed on to preach to the passersby like he did every morning.

I waved. I didn't have time for Sandman this morning, but I needed to see what he wore. It had to be something from the sixties or seventies. He didn't rock today's gear or any teeth.

"Youngin', I say. Come here." He was waving his hand, getting louder with each word. He stomped his dusty wing-tipped foot, and almost fell off of the crate.

I shook my head, laughing. I decided I'd go and give him some respect. He was the one who made stuff happen for me—for a price—like my vending license I'm too young to have.

"What's up, Sandman?" I asked, checking out his peach suit with purple pinstripes, and a blue flower in his lapel. Sure enough, his collar was long enough to reach his chest. No lie.

"Teaching. Preaching. And I tell you, youngin', don't let these streets eat you alive. In Harlem only the strong survive. You better listen to what I say, I'm Sandman, the official unofficial mayor of Harlem. I don't play. These young girls walking these streets with strollers, snitching on themselves about the beat they danced to nine-months ago with boys who aren't going *no*where. Watch 'em, youngin'. They'll steal your dreams . . . and I'm not talking about the fast girls or the young daddies. I'm talking about the babies. There's poison in their formula."

"Gotcha, Sandman. Thanks for the wisdom of the day." I walked away before he could give me any more of his version of knowledge, and gripped my bag. I made it to the other side without a scratch or hiccup. I had to go to school, but I also had to check on my vending table to make sure merchandise was stocked, and my brother, Broke-up, who had had more broken bones than anyone I'd ever known, had singles for change.

"What 'appened, Z? Don't tell me you ah skip sk-ewl dis marn-nin?" Broke-up asked with a West Indian accent way thicker than mine. It was something he brought back with him from Jamaica every year after spending the summer there with our grandmother, while I worked slanging knockoff designer bags and bootleg CDs.

"Dis Sodom and Gomorrah!" he said, cutting his eyes at a guy who was wearing skinny jeans, and a fitted Alvin Ailey T-shirt, and had a pair of ballet slippers wrapped around his neck like jewelry. The dude was a dancer, a very good one I'd seen perform on many occasions.

"You see that, Z?" Broke-up asked, sucked his teeth, and then spat. "Dis world sick. Just sick. What kind of man walk around like dat? Him no girl. What he wear tights pants for, not for de women. Dat's why men should not dance."

I almost answered and agreed with his nonsense like usual so I wouldn't give myself away, but this girl caught my eye with her thickness. I could only see her from the back, but that was good enough.

"English, Broke-up. English. You're not on the island anymore."

"Yeah. Yeah. A'ight. But just so you know, I'm going to be selling my music. Cool?" he asked, switching back to his New York accent without problem.

"Yeah. Cool," I answered him, my eyes still on the girl's thickness. "Psst. Psst. Can I talk to you for a minute?" I asked her from behind. "Maybe buy you breakfast, beautiful?"

The girl looked over her shoulder, and my stomach dropped.

Dang.

"Z, you're full of it. You already 'talked' to me." She bunny-eared her fingers and made air quotes. "Talked and talked and talked. Then you wouldn't call back."

I turned my head like I didn't see her. I didn't have time for shorty. But her sister . . . now *she* was a whole different story. She was Caribbean thick with Cooley hair, and the girl was smart. Now her—the sister—*she* could get it. Something serious. Any time of the day or night. I waved my hand in the air, telling the girl to push on. "So Broke-up, you got this, right? I'm not going to be able to pay attention in class if I have to worry about you and this table."

Broke-up yawned, then laughed. "G'won, Z! I got this.

You think I don't know how to hold down the vending table, eh? Let me break it down for you, Star. . . ."

I raised my eyebrows. No, I didn't think he could manage, but I didn't have a choice. I had to go to school. Had to get my Savion Glover and Alvin Ailey and Fred Astaire on so I could eventually choreograph videos and concerts for top-billing stars. Broke-up, on the other hand, didn't have nothing to do, nowhere to go, and no dream to achieve. He also had no idea I was a dancer. No one in my family or on my block knew, and I was going to keep it like that. I was all male; I wouldn't give them the chance to question my sexuality or massacre my bravado. That's what they'd do if they had an idea because where I came from, unless you were winding with some girl, you didn't dance. Dancing was for batty boys, homosexual men. And I sure wasn't one. I loved females. All of them, girls and women. But thick ones . . . yeah . . . they were my weakness.

". . . and Coach bags are over here. One for fifty, two for eighty. And on this other side we have the music. Remixes. Rap. R and B. Reggae. Calypso. Dancehall." He was still talking.

I pulled twenty-three singles out of my pocket, the only money to my name, and gave him eighteen.

"You need singles to make change, Broke-up. I'll catch you later."

I was across the street, and headed to the train before he could stop talking. I had to get to school early so I could get a position up front. Mrs. Allen was the director and she didn't take no mess. She was also the one with the connects. And I needed to be connected ASAP, so I had to show her I was serious. Plus, I needed to see the selection of females that Harlem Academy had to offer. I crossed my fingers and asked Jah to bless me with some thick ones. Wasn't nothing like thick girls, good food, and dancing. And I was hungry for all three.

JAMAICA-KINCAID ELLISON

"I can act my way into and out of anything."

I sat in front of the tiny television with my eyes glued to the screen and my fingers crossed. Every day the torment grew worse and upped my anxiety. How was I going to keep pulling this off?

"By acting my way through it, of course," I said to myself, then finally exhaled when the morning news went off. I was so wrapped up in thinking that today was the day my picture was going to float across the screen with *missing* or *runaway* under it, that I hadn't even realized I'd been holding my breath.

"Okay. This is it. The day of all days. The day my life changes," I pep-talked myself, and unfolded my body from its Indian-style crossed legged position on the floor.

My computer rang from the attached speakers, and my heart stopped. My hands started sweating and I could feel the flush rising to my hairline. I could do this. I knew this moment was coming, just as it had every first day of school for the last four years. Stepping over my pallet on the floor, I crossed the room to the makeshift table I'd assembled out of discarded milk crates that I'd borrowed from the store, then accepted the incoming call and sat in front of the screen. My mother's face blurred as it popped up on the screen. As usual, she was too close to the camera, and I knew without her speaking she'd be talking too loud. My parents were stuck in time, technophobes who could never get technology right. I smirked. If they weren't vegans, I'm sure they'd yell into drive-thru speakers at fast-food restaurants.

"Good morning, Mother!" I greeted her, overly chipper. Being positive was a must-do in my family. There was no room for mediocrity of any kind, even if you felt that way.

"Good morning, Jamaica. Can you see me? Do you hear me?"

I could see the blur of her milky skin, and catch a glimpse of her always-perfect makeup and diamond earrings that were large enough to fund a small third-world country's hungry children for months, maybe years.

"Brad, honey. I don't think Jamaica can see me. I do believe it's time we have someone go to the school and set up audiovisual like on the set. . . ."

Hunh?! Panic started to roll in immediately. I didn't need audiovisual or them sending their people to make my space look like the Oprah Winfrey set—the same set my television-star dad had replicated because anything Oprah did had to be the best. My Mac was just fine, and Skype was great. I didn't need anything for my dorm room because, though they had no idea, I wasn't tucked in one at the ritzy boarding school I'd been shuttled off to at eleven years old. I'd forged their signatures, all but emptied my bank accounts, paid my sister to keep quiet, and rented me this nightmare of a studio apartment that I absolutely loved, then enrolled at Harlem Academy as soon as I'd been accepted.

"I can see you just fine, Mother. How's the beauty line coming?" I asked, to throw her off topic and onto the one that was her favorite: her.

"The line is amazing. Did I tell you that we have stars wearing us now? We were mentioned at the Oscars. Great press . . ." She finally quieted, and I knew there was a problem. "Jamaica, is that a . . . *what* is that behind you? Your dorm room is hideous this year." She put her hand on the camera, trying to cover it, but I could still see her turn to my dad. "Brad, I think we need to go there and speak to someone. Jamaica's roughing it."

"Mother! Mother!" I shouted. "This is a temporary room that I'm studying in. The private study rooms are full," I lied.

"How about a study trailer, Jamaica? You know with the right attitude, environment, and belief there's nothing you can't accomplish with a bit of hard work." My dad took his turn in front of the camera now. He wore his perpetual smile, and was in full motivational guru mode.

"I'm fine, Dad. Really. I don't need a camera set, a study trailer, or anything. All I want is to go to school and be *normal* . . . and see you guys at Christmas, like always." I swept my blond dreaded locks from my face, and accidentally brushed the piercing under my lip, then rethought my normal statement. "I just want to be me. Okay?"

He clapped his hands together. "Christmas it is! But to make your mother feel better, we're going to wire money into your sister's account so she can help you purchase a car. She's eighteen now, so she can do it without us being there. We're going to computer call her now. Love you, Jamaica. Over and out." The connection went dead.

I finally relaxed, knowing somehow and someway, I'd be able to pull off my charade for a few months without them knowing I'd moved to New York, ditched their idea of prep school to prepare my way into the field of acting. I knew I'd just have to keep being the actor who lived inside me to make it work.

My stomach growled angrily. Without thought, I made my way to the barely a sneeze of a kitchenette, and opened the refrigerator. Bare, except for the bottled water. I shrugged and opened a cabinet, and took out my last pack of sixty-cent cookies. They'd have to do because it was all I had, and I'd told myself to get used to it. I was "roughing it" as my mother had said, and I knew it wasn't going to change. They could deposit all the money into my sister's account that they wanted, but I knew I wouldn't see a dime of it. It'd be hers as payment for keeping her mouth sealed. And I'd have to go out and try to find a job to support myself. But what could I do? I was the daughter of a supermodel mother and disgustingly rich motivational guru dad. I didn't know what it meant to be born with a silver spoon in my mouth. Our spoons were platinum. But to go to the Harlem Academy and breathe life into my dreams, I'd settle for plastic sporks.

Dreams were classless; it didn't matter what your socioeconomic background was. And they were also colorless—I hoped. Because I knew for sure that in Harlem, I'd be the minority. The white girl with blond dreadlocks who would stop at nothing to not only thrive, but belong.